STORIES AND SYMMETRIES

Part I

Joshua Kepfer

ACKNOWLEDGMENTS

Thank you, Mom, Dad, Jamie, Jess, Jimmy, and Madeleine, for your advice and support.

Thank you, Sam, for going first.

Thank You, Jesus Christ. You know why.

CONTENTS

INTRODUCTION

Since no one reads introductions, I'll be able to give away my secrets.

Symmetry can be found almost everywhere in the universe. Nature is flooded with it. Galaxies, planets, plants, animals, humans—all of us exhibit some form of symmetry. In nature, a symmetrical system is often the most efficient—the path of least resistance, but I think symmetry points to something deeper than this.

As the Russian poet Alexander Pushkin put it, "Symmetry is a characteristic of the human mind."

Humans crave symmetry. We are constantly looking for a more balanced, efficient, and beautiful way of doing things. We are very keen on finding patterns almost anywhere. Numbers, pictures, music, but what about words?

This is one reason I wrote this book, to show some of the symmetry that can be found in words, stories, and ideas.

Another reason is that I'm bored. I'm bored of people coming up with the same books, music, movies, and art. Old ideas that are all re-hashed and re-done. You won't find that here. What you will find is something fresh.

This book is comprised of poetry and stories, of which some may take two hours to read, some only thirty seconds. Some were written years ago when I was in quite a different place, some were written only months prior to publication.

The poems are special. They have very unique, symmetric qualities, which is why I like to call them Symmetries. Each of these Symmetries will have multiple messages, depending on how you read them. And no, I am not just talking about metaphors and figurative language.

The fiction has symmetry as well. Some of this is physical symmetry, some is more abstract.

You might find symmetry hidden between objects, characters, themes, or even the words themselves.

Rather than give everything away, I'll let you figure it out. It's like a little game we'll get to play as you read. But don't worry, if you are unable to solve a puzzle, the answer will often be on the page after it.

MERCY

In the silence of the forest, a man is bent over, retying his son's dangling bootlaces. The son bites his lip. Father had already shown him how to tie them properly once. The man stands up, and walks ahead of his son, saying nothing.

Son follows with his head lowered, but soon regains the excitement of joining his father for the first time. He has a hard time keeping up with the pace while trying to match his steps with the faint imprints Father's boots stamp on the leaves and mud. Father stops, and Son runs into him before he notices. The man's sure eyes glare at his son's until he knows he will pay attention, and then he points to the ground. Son looks at where he is pointing, then back up at him, blank. Father sighs and kneels down, laying aside his rifle, and continues to point. Son looks closer now and sees what could be an animal footprint. The father makes his other hand like claws, and mouths, "Wolf," then puts his index finger in front of his closed lips.

At the word *wolf,* Son lets out a quick gasp, then clamps a hand to his mouth and resumes his ashamed posture. But he notices something else in the mud and points to it. Father takes interest and studies the miniature version of the other paw print. He smiles at his son and rubs his hair.

Father stands up with the assistance of his rifle, and Son stands too, a little straighter this time. They continue, more cautiously than before, but they do not get far before a noise startles them, a menacing growl from not far away. Both of them dart their eyes around. The father spots a wolf and whips his rifle toward it, pulling back the hammer. He should shoot right now but needs to be careful. If he misses a vital point, he will have to reload which takes too long. He steps in front of his son.

The wolf is a female, gray and black, with eyes that desire blood. Most of her sharp, yellow teeth are visible in the snarl. She steps in front of her small cub, the only one unaware of the present danger.

Son sees the cub and tugs his father's coat and says, "Wait."

"Quiet," Father orders, but he decides to listen to his son's request. They slowly back away from the beast. The wolf continues a little toward them, still growling, but then gives up and runs off with her cub.

Father lets out an audible breath and relaxes his arms. Son does not relax as easily.

"Close call," Father says, "they are probably heading back to their den. If we go further east, we should steer clear of them." He starts marching forward, then warns, "No one lives after approaching a wolf den."

Son hesitates to follow after the scare. He wants to go home and sit with Mother by the fire, but he does not say that.

Father looks at him, "Are you all right?"

"Yes," Son says with a brave face.

"I know that must have been a frightening experience for you, but we need to keep moving. We haven't seen a single deer, not even a rabbit yet."

Son catches up. "I'm glad we didn't shoot them."

"We got lucky. Nature does not reward mercy."

They keep silent for thirty more minutes until they find a creek. After filling up water and chewing on dried meat, they continue and arrive at a large meadow. Trudging through the middle of it, they search for any hints of life in the tall grass. This goes on for a while until they come to a large grouping of rocks. Boulders are stacked on top of each other in such a way that the areas in between them would make adequate caves. Son's first impression is that the structure looks very fun to climb, but is surprised by Father's reaction.

Father nudges Son backward, and he obeys. Some noises come from one of the caves, and a wolf comes out that Son recognizes. The same cub also follows its mother and mimics her, sniffing in the air for something, but the mother growls at it and nudges it back inside. The wind blows from behind the humans, and the wolf catches the scent and turns in their direction. Son can see the aggression in her movement from this distance. Father looks very concerned, but his coat makes a good shield, and Son clings to it as tightly as he can.

An angry howl sounds.

They continue to retrace their footsteps, faster. "I should have killed it, I knew I should have," Father says, but then regrets the statement.

Another wolf comes bounding out of the cave, this one clearly a male. Several others follow, all full-grown, barking, snarling and howling. Father loses all hope. They had stumbled upon a den.

He fires a shot in the air, a loud crack. The wolves jerk in different directions, startled, but resume their angles of attack. Father fumbles to reload the single-shot Remington as the wolves fan out to surround their invaders.

Father knows that he will not be able to kill more than two of them with his rifle. The nearest line of trees is over a hundred yards away, there is no way they can both outrun the wolves. The father looks at his son, then to the trees, then to his rifle, and closes his eyes.

Son is terrified and looks in his father's face for comfort, but his father is in the middle of making a very hard decision, and there is no comfort there.

Then Father opens his eyes, takes a deep, shuddering breath, and places the gun in his boy's hands, and says, "We can't both make it. Run."

"What?"

"They will chase me, and when they do, you need to run. If they come after you, climb a tree."

"I can't," Son tries to give the gun back.

Father pushes the heavy rifle back onto Son, "You only have time for one shot, make it count," and then he sprints toward the pack of wolves before his son can see the tears on his face.

"Dad!" Son shouts.

"Leave!"

When fathers use that tone, sons react on instinct. Son turns and runs away but looks back once he reaches the trees. The wolves are huddled in a circle in the tall grass, no longer chasing anyone. His father is not visible anymore.

He steadies his arm and aims the rifle at the pack. Father had only just taught him how to shoot. He pulls the trigger and feels a thundering shock, but it does not hit any of the targets. The wolves are startled and then go back to feasting.

If he had only kept his mouth shut in the forest.

He turns around and runs all the way home.

The return feels like it is not real, like a dream. The weight of the gun becomes burdensome, but he never loosens his grip on it, not even when he arrives at home and sits by the fire with Mother. He finally cries in her arms, but Mother does not understand the full reason.

LOVE AND SACRIFICE

This love is full of
Life and cheer
Is this not why we
Sacrifice
To not let go of
Those we hold
Who teach us to know
Love and joy
But what we may find
Is not true
Pointless are feelings
To distract
Those we cannot hide
Who loves you
Don't sacrifice them

This poem has a syllable rhythm of 5-3-5-3, which is symmetric, but that's not why it's a Symmetry. Reading the first word of each line down vertically reveals another sentence, which happens to be the theme of the poem.

This	love is full of
life	and cheer
is	this not why we
sacrifice	
to	not let go of
those	we hold
who	teach us to know
love,	and joy
but	what we may find
is	not true
pointless	are feelings
to	distract
those	we cannot hide
who	loves you
don't.	sacrifice them

UNASHAMED, UNAPOLOGETIC, AND UNRELENTING

I was walking from 5th to 9th, not a long hike. Taxi was at a red light, traffic was horrible, so walking would be faster at this point. I got out of the car and tipped the driver.

"You got somewhere to be?" He said.

I grinned, "It's karaoke night."

Open air is always so refreshing after work. I felt more alive after every step I took. The atmosphere at Brad's can be a little stuffy, so this was a good opportunity to enjoy the cold breeze before I got in. But I never made it to Brad's that night.

About halfway there, in front of the Chinese place, I got stopped. No one stopped me on purpose, I just saw something that made me forget about the open air, forget about singing. I don't know why what I saw affected me so much. Other people kept walking right past without a second glance, as they should have, it was none of our business. On the edge of the curb under a streetlamp, I saw a couple standing there. The back of the man's coat was turned to me, but the woman was facing toward me. She wore a long jacket, a red scarf, and gloves.

What got to me was the face, it was all I could see. She was probably in her thirties, maybe forties, it was hard to tell, but she was crying. She had her chin scrunched on the guy's shoulder, and she was just bawling. The two of them weren't making any noise, just hugging and crying together. There were so many tears, it looked like it was raining on only the right shoulder of his jacket.

I've seen plenty of sad faces before, plenty adults cry, but for some reason, this woman was by far the worst I've ever seen. I cannot authentically describe how sad she looked. Her lips were all twisted, her face was red, below her nose mixed snot with the tears. There was barely any make-up left on her face to wash down. Underneath all this ugliness and pain, there was somehow a beauty visible in her face.

Her eyes were looking down at the sidewalk when I first saw them, but then she looked at me. Straight into my eyes, into my heart, and she didn't look away. She was not sorry for how this made me feel. I couldn't tear my eyes away from hers. They were red and puffy from all the crying, but still somehow feminine and beautiful. I don't know how long I stood staring at her, and I don't know why I did for that long. I thought that they would be done in a minute, so we could all move on with our lives.

Eventually, she turned, and they walked away, hands clasped. It was so abrupt, I was unsure of what I was supposed to do next. I turned around and walked back. I couldn't go to Brad's, I couldn't sing after seeing that. I walked all the way home, imagining what could have happened to make her that sad. Even trying not to think about it, I couldn't stop. Her face was tattooed in my mind.

I figured out on that walk why I might have stopped there, why I was willing to let her tear me away from my contentment. I looked up to this woman.

I've seen a lot of people going through shit, I mean really going through it: parents died, spouse died, abused, raped. I'm friends with some of these kinds of people, and the similarity in all of them is emptiness. Their faces shut down, especially in public. Their eyes get dim, their lips are flat, eyebrows are neither up nor down, all expression is gone. The face of this woman on the street had none of those qualities, yet she was as sad as any person can be. She didn't run from her grief, she ran toward it. She didn't escape her pain, she embraced it in a way that I'm terrified to.

Unashamed.

Unapologetic.

Unrelenting.

That's who I want to be.

§

"Beauty is rather a light that plays over the symmetry
of things than that symmetry itself."

–Plotinus

§

AISHA

Those who knew her knew her as Shelly. I get why she changed her name, but it didn't help the way she intended it to. Her real name was Aisha Kharobi. People didn't need to know that fact to feel uncomfortable around her. When she wore her hijab, they knew she was a Muslim. They heard her speak and knew she came from somewhere in the Middle East. They saw her skin and subconsciously associated her with terrorists. She got rid of both the veil and the name and improved her accent, but skin color is a more difficult problem to fix.

Aisha was the name of one of the prophet Muhammad's many wives. Taking her was an act of charity, he asserted, since she was an orphan, and family. She was six years old when they were married, and nine at most when they consummated. Muhammad had sex with a nine-year-old named Aisha.

Our Aisha's parents told her not to share her name with any Americans, they would not understand, but she was surprised when she arrived in the U.S. and found that none of the Americans cared what her first name was, or meant. Ancient history did not matter to them as much as recent history.

Then, as years passed, the miraculous happened, and I started to see more and more Americans treating Aisha like an American, no different from anyone else. She wasn't so scared to be in public anymore.

I remember being with her at a coffee shop, and this girl started talking to us. If she was at all stereotyping Aisha—Shelly—she gave no hint of it, nor of over-compensating for her ignorance. It was refreshing. Shelly was even bold enough to disagree with her at an appropriate time. The girl was saying how intolerant and corrupt American society was getting.

"Well, actually, some countries that I've heard of are much more corrupt than America," Shelly shyly stated, "and as intolerant as Americans are, Islamic countries are more so."

"How do you know?" the white girl said, "Can't you see all the sexism, racism, and privilege of white men around here?" She spread her arms out and gestured around her.

"Maybe, but Muslim women don't have any rights of their own. They can't talk or work or drive or do anything without a man giving them permission first."

"Really?" Conviction hit the white girl's face for a few seconds.

"Yes, it's horrible over there."

"No, it's just a very different culture." She resumed her enlightened state.

"You don't understand, women are legally raped there."

"I do understand, and men get away with that all the time here, too."

"It's different. My—I know people who lived there, and they were suffering a lot."

"That's because of war, not religion. And people suffer everywhere. I'm saying here, no one's even doing anything about it."

"It's still better than Islam. Anything is better than Islam."

"How can you say that about someone else's religion? Just because they're different. This is exactly what I'm talking about, everyone is intolerant of everything now. That's their culture over there, you can't just hate on them."

"No, but—" she became silent. I expected Shelly to take off her disguise and tell her who she really was then, but she didn't. She just sat there staring at the table.

The white girl gave a victorious, I-feel-sorry-for-you smirk and walked off with her soy latte to change the world somewhere else.

"How could you let her walk away without telling her where you're from?" I asked.

Watery tears formed in her pink eyes. "It shouldn't matter where I'm from. How do they not see how terrible Islam is? Why would anyone want to defend that?"

By her last question, she had dropped into her Saudi accent again and got a few confused glances from around the café.

MIRROR

Mirror your view to shift the effect. Search the ending to get help to process the change. Answer that back to yourself for enough evidence to build and support your construct. Construct your support and build to evidence enough for yourself to back that answer. Change the process to help get to ending the search. Effect the shift to view your mirror.

This Symmetry has the same words repeated in the opposite order halfway through. You can start from the last word and read backwards to get the same paragraph. Pretty cool, huh? It's like a palindrome, but with words, not letters.

WOMAN IN THE WOOD

Look at this lonely wood, how it sways and bends, creaks and snaps. See it sleep, and breathe. An ancient, steady wall of trees overlooking a flowering meadow, backed by tall, grey mountains. See the animals play in this field: crickets and deer, beetles and skunks, butterflies and sparrows all hunting, sniffing, flying and leaping, but rarely do they go into the woods. The forest, their home, but they seem reluctant to enter when their time comes. There can be seen a caution in their steps as dusk approaches. Why is this, many people wonder, what could cause such a disturbance with nature?

If one were to delve into this mystery, the first object that would likely capture one's attention would be the tree. Not quite as tall as the other oaks or pines, but once the eye spots it, it is difficult to look away. Across the meadow, near the beginning of the line of trees, there is a vacancy; a hole in nature, as if nothing desires to grow in the soil besides this single tree.

Thin, pale bark clasping unbroken on the trunk with silver, pointed, untamed leaves surrounding it. The tree looks unnatural, unbalanced, like it knows not where it belongs. If one were to begin to move close to the tree, uneasiness would fill the person's stomach, especially when sunlight is seen reflected off its bleached leaves. Beautiful, or just unusual, one would ponder; pure, or demonic?

There was a time when people might have walked through these woods in Southern Germany, when the warnings were subtler. Only two people were ever known to explore this portion of it. Coincidentally, they were both within a year of each other.

The first was Melanie Seidel, who happened upon it as she was strolling down a path to her village. She was walking back from the market like she usually did on autumn evenings, but it happened that on this autumn evening she was alone. This was unusual; ladies had escorts almost everywhere they went, and she gladly accepted this courtesy once she became of courting age.

When she was a child, however, she would run and play for hours by herself. No one knew where she was, or what she was up to. Now, as the lady saw this wood, perhaps it was the childlike spirit in her that drew her away from safety, perhaps it was a gust of wind that turned her face to the trees, but whatever the reason, she left the trodden path and headed toward the dark wood. It was in the middle of autumn this night, and with a fresh rain just past, there was a marvelous twinkling on the forest wherever the moonlight touched the dew on the leaves or grass. A field of wild grain lay between her and her forest. It took three minutes to cross in her trance-like march to the edge of the trees.

When Melanie arrived there, she stopped, as if waking again. *Why haven't I heard of anyone ever entering this wood,* she wondered. She found it difficult to move forward now, and her heart was thumping harshly. Her legs tried to turn back, but still she stood, gazing into the murky, dark green. Something in this wood was so alluring, unique, and magical, she could not look away. The land had been in a drought for a time, yet this wood seemed to have kept all its vitality. The air fresher, the leaves untrod, the colors brighter. Even at dusk, she could see into it quite clearly. No broken branch, no sign of animals, not even a bird settling in its nest. She dared a step, and then three more. All was silent aside from her unrhythmic breaths.

Then, with young eyes bulging, she treaded among the trees. With each passing step, she found this place to be more and more tranquil, and she grew excited. She felt free here: unhindered by any of the troubles and chores of her village. Melanie started to run, then dance, then skip, then laugh, then shout, faster and louder as she went. She ended up in a meadow, dizzy and delighted. She laid there for a while, completely content as she was, with cool grass under her hot fingertips, and scented air soothing her aching chest.

Eventually, her eye caught a tree that looked different than all the others. No, gladly, not the haunting tree described before, but a thick, gnarly oak, or was it a willow, that stood alone in an otherwise dense thicket of trees. Curiosity won her, and she waltzed over to this tree, but her pace slowed as she came closer, contrary to the thumping in her chest. Long drapes of white webs hung down from its many branches and swayed along with the wind. *Tillandsia usneoides*, Spanish Moss, she knew nothing about it other than the ghostly impression it gave her, like dead beards hanging from the tree. She plucked up the courage to duck between the moss, but she hesitated to touch the tree, now that it was so close. Such an old, rough, and lonely tree it looked. Trembling, she laid a hand on the trunk.

At that instant, she heard something that sounded like an old man sighing. She turned in every direction looking for the source of the strange noise, but there were no humans around her. Everything was silent now, and she dared not even to breathe. *What if this wood is haunted?* Melanie hadn't taken five strides away from the tree when she heard someone say, "Do not go." Obediently, she froze, hoping her fears were untrue. She sensed the words, felt them, more than heard them.

"You touched me," the noise continued.

Afraid of punishment, the Meanie spoke in return, "Yes, I did. I am sorry that I troubled you."

"Trouble?" The slow voice sounded, "What trouble could a hand cause me?" Laughter vibrated from the ground around her. "I was sleeping, and I felt the touch of human's flesh. I had not felt this touch since I was youthful." She didn't know what to do, but to stand and pray. "You bring good memories to me, child. Thank you."

The girl felt gratitude tingling up her legs, and flashes of calm and peace soothed into her. She stood there for moments looking at the leaves above. Then she decided to slide her hand down the trunk once again. There was a loud cracking in the tree, like it was letting go of tension. It must have been a beautiful sight, this woman standing by the White Oak, *Quercus alba*. The tree let Melanie climb up and sit in its sturdy branches, and they conversed about many things until she fell asleep.

It wasn't until the morning light seeped into her sleeping eyes that Melanie remembered her home. She jumped out of the tree and ran through the woods, but then realized she did not know which direction her village was. At every angle she looked, the forest seemed the same. Panic started to grip her. She circled frantically for a whole day until she came to the meadow by the large tree again. The familiar sight comforted her, and she decided that it wouldn't be too bad to stay here, just for a little while longer.

The Oak told her all it knew: how to find and store food, where to find running water, how to plant new trees, but not how to find her home. She wandered and explored, but never found the way back. After some time, she stopped searching, and her old village and family began to feel like dreams and distant memories.

Over the months, she would see few animals that one would normally glimpse in a healthy wood. The only sounds she heard became music to her: the falling of leaves, the wind sifting through treetops, and the light beat of her feet on the soft grass. She did not dislike the lack of beasts. In fact, she grew to feel less closely related to animals as she did with trees, specifically Old Oak. This odd relationship only increased, and each day she was in the wood brought her and the tree closer together. It would be almost a full year before she met another human again. The chill of winter, the freshness of spring, the warmth of summer, these were truly wonderful days, while they lasted.

* * *

The second person to enter this wood was very unlike the first. This one was a man. Tall, bearded, and intimidating, a man of renown in his community. His profession was hard labor, anything people needed a strong, simple man for: building, guarding, moving furniture, woodcutting. He was an exceptional woodcutter and boasted that there was no tree he could not single-handedly fell. No one doubted his claims.

His experience in the wood was much shorter than

Melanie's. He entered through the opposite side, across from the meadow, and he too wondered at its apparent vacancy. There were rumors: intelligent trees, a witch who roamed the woods, people lost in its maze, *but did people really believe those stories?* He didn't in the least and was determined to conquer this wood and show the lies in these myths. So, he hiked down to the meadow one day with only his trusted axe for unneeded protection, but uneasiness tingled on his fingertips as he approached the trees. He had an urge to return to the security of his town, but he had a stronger desire to prove himself. Then it caught his eye: the space not far away where no trees existed in a ten-yard radius around a single oak, thrice the width of any others.

What could cause this oddity? It was as if the other trees were afraid of this one. And he could almost understand why. This tree looked thick, tangled, ancient, and menacing. Long webs of Spanish Moss hung down from its far-reaching branches. *If any tree deserves to be chopped down,* thought the man, *it must be this one.* He would chop it down and leave with an impressive branch as a victory. That way he would not have to go deep into the woods to uncover mysteries, which was something he did not decrease to dread.

He walked to the tree and swung his axe. Immediately, he wanted to stop. The tree seemed to feel the wound. Guilt was gnawing at the man's stomach, but he kept swinging. Hours later, the job was finally done, and no easy job it was. It took the strong man all day to hew the thick oak down, leaving him exhausted and sweaty, sitting on the stump he had made. That is where the howl, the penetrating scream fell upon his ears.

Melanie saw him swing the last stroke, saw the tree crack and fall hopelessly to ground. But she felt, more than saw. The thump of the heavy blade contacting the oak hurt as if it had stopped her own heart. She lost control of her mind then and did what instinct forced her to do. She raced straight toward the man who had just killed the thing she loved. She screamed, and the startled man turned to see her.

The axeman was by no means cowardly, but he still found it difficult to stomach the sight of the ragged woman running at him. He decided to face his fear, and stood upon his stump, readying his axe to meet the freakish woman who was unquestionably the witch rumored about.

There was a lengthy patch of blackberry brambles in between them, which put the man more at ease. She would have to go around 200 meters to reach him, but the man did not understand how easily hate can displace a sound mind. The female was not turning, and she was gaining speed toward the bush, and then, to his astonishment, she jumped straight into the sea of thorns. She landed right in the middle of it. Her skinny form slid through all the way up to her neck. When she screamed again, he knew it was not only from the pain. Her bloodthirsty eyes never left his. She scrambled, pushed, and tore her way through the thorny branches.

The woodcutter had never been so frightened in his life. Truly, what was before him was the most distressing thing a man can see: real, unhindered madness increased by raw, unfiltered hate. He knew she was a witch now, not because of her wildness, or tattered clothes, but because of the last, worst detail, the smile on her face.

When she wriggled out of the thorns' last grasp, there were gashes and cuts all over her body and thorns still stuck in her skin, but she hardly lost a step.

The man lost his confidence. He wasn't sure why the witch even wanted to attack him, but his instinct told him that he was going to die if he fought her. This knowledge became increasingly powerful as the female got closer. The mad eyes, the harsh scream, the resoluteness, it was too much for the man, and he turned to flee. But then it was too late, he should have run at the first sight of this woman.

She leaped onto him before he left the line of trees. The axe slipped from his sweaty hand as they both tumbled to the ground. She bit his neck like a wild wolf, and he flung her off of him, spraining her ankle, and tried to flee again. She was on him again in seconds, hitting, slapping, pulling, scraping, biting, she went wild on the poor man. The intense struggle went on for a while as the once intimidating, powerful man was being beaten by a crazed woman. A last desperate attempt to save himself was made.

"I'm sorry!" he screamed, but she did not listen. The woman kept waling on him and tried to strangle the man with her petite hands. This was too difficult, so she picked up the disoriented man's axe and swung it into his gut, and then all was silent.

A deep depression then replaced the revenge in her, and she slumped back to her tree and laid down on the trunk. Her hands held the strong branch she had once slept on. Her fingertips could feel its life draining. The steady, pulsing breath became just a ripple of energy, soon to be extinguished. She was perplexed at what else she felt, though. There was not much anger, or regret, or depression in this tree, but acceptance. Then it finally died. No more energy, no more intimacy, only wood spread out on the dirt.

No! she surged with all her energy, *you cannot die!* And she noticed its acorns scattered about her. These could replace the tree, but they would need a damp environment, and this land was still in a drought. A trickle of hope entered her crazed mind. What if the man really was sorry for killing her love? What if he could still make his amends? The girl rushed to find the tall man's axe. She struck the ground with it and loosened the earth. Then she furiously dug out enough dirt to make a shallow grave and dragged the broken man into it. She then swung the axe down on the corpse's chest. Ribs gave way to the sharp edge, leaving a cavity in the middle of its chest. She reached in and grabbed out the heart. Disgusted, she threw the thing away for the birds to eat. In its place, she put the most perfect acorn that she had ever seen; long, round, ideal for germination. She buried the man with hope in her own heart. "If you are truly sorry, then make me a tree," she said, and then drifted down from exhaustion. Just before she fell asleep, she worriedly murmured, "But what if you don't want to."

When the woman awoke, she did something possibly stranger than the last day. She took up the axe and dug another hole about five feet from the original one. She gently picked up a new acorn and wondered at its beauty. The female then lay down in the grave she had made. She kissed the acorn like a mother would kiss her own child and placed it on top of her heart. Then she began to bury herself with the dirt she had placed around the hole. Who knows why she did this? Maybe she was unsure of the first plan, maybe she wanted to mother the tree herself, maybe this man couldn't save the tree, what if he didn't want it enough? Whatever the reason was, the female fell unconscious there in that hole she dug, and she never moved again.

Months later, the sprout of a new tree came up above ground for the first time. In the middle of a drought, the sickly, bleached oak was conceived. It can be looked upon as a warning to all who venture there that this wood is unnatural and should not be neared. All who hear this story wonder, but none are ever sure, whether it was from the man that this tree was made, or the woman. Was it required for the seed the blood of a murderer, or love from a bride?

§

Again, nature is flooded with symmetry. This applies to human nature as much as it does the natural realm.

§

LIFE AND DEATH

Reasons for what humans hope for in death,
For survival is that which our body fails.
Living and dying are both shells in life.
Are we over showing need outside our speaking?
Not all the possibilities life presents will be.
All love living and progress death even still.

Reasons for living are not all
for survival. And we all love
what is dying over the living
humans that are showing possibilities and
hope, which both need life. Progress
for our shells outside presents death
in body. In our will, even
death fails life, speaking be still.

In this Symmetry, the second stanza has exactly the same words as the first. I just flipped it on its side. It's easier to see in a grid.

Reasons	for	what	humans	hope	for	in	death,
for	survival	is	that	which	our	body	fails.
Living	and	dying	are	both	shells	in	life.
Are	we	over	showing	need	outside	our	speaking?
Not	all	the	possibilities	life	presents	will	be.
All	love	living	and	progress	death	even	still.

Reasons	for	living	are	not	all
for	survival.	And	we	all	love
what	is	dying	over	the	living
humans	that	are	showing	possibilities	and
hope,	which	both	need	life.	Progress
for	our	shells	outside	presents	death
in	body.	In	our	will,	even
death	fails	life,	speaking	be	still.

DUMAN ELEMENTARY 1ST GRADERS

School is different from what I remember it being. First off, why do all parents have to be so egotistical when it comes to their kids? I don't care if your child is on the honor roll or the soccer team, they are not special. Neither are you, for that matter. You're an average to bad parent just like the rest of us. You're not fooling anyone.

I'll give an example: the talent show. How could one forget the magical Duman Elementary annual 1st grade talent show? I want to know whose genius idea it was to make a talent show for little children.

Aw, 1st graders, so cute, right? Think again.

I don't care if they did well or not, most at least tried. What I have a problem with is the parents comparing their kids with each other. That just makes the parents feel better about themselves and the kids feel worse. They're in the 1st grade, they all suck. The most talented of them are at a low 2nd grade level, at best.

The magical evening was hosted by the vice-principal. This was her big night to shine. She was gunning for principal next year, everyone knew it. I followed my son into the dimly lit multi-purpose room, and he disappeared behind the stage, leaving me bored and alone in the sea of mingling parents. Smooth jazz was playing in the background, complete with punch and hors d'oeuvres. She was serving *hors d'oeuvres* at the 1st grade talent show. I even found myself scanning the room for a cocktail bar at one point.

All the kids were behind the curtain dealing with their stress, while their parents were out here bragging about them, or themselves, with each other. I didn't feel like joining. I was about to go find a seat when all of a sudden something three feet high collided with me. I turned around.

"Woah, you okay there?" I asked and helped the little girl to her feet. She was wearing a pink dress that looked like a life-size replica of a barbie outfit or something.

"No," she said, crying, "I need to find my mom. All the other girls have makeup, but I don't have any!"

I looked around. No one else even noticed her.

"You know where your mom is?"

She shook her head, crying even more.

"Hey, hey, it's okay. Here," I said, and grabbed a

napkin to dab her tears. "There. You look beautiful. You don't need that makeup stuff anyways."

"Yes I do," she sniffed.

"No, you'll outshine the rest of them, no doubt in my mind. Let's go find your mom. What's her name?"

"Linda," she said, and she instinctively gripped my hand as we walked around the expansive room.

"I'm Brody's dad," I said, "you know Brody?"

She nodded her head. The crying had stopped at least.

After yelling *Linda* for the seventh time, a woman turned her head to us. I could see her expression go all the way from confused to startled to upset to feigned gratefulness on her way over.

"Oh, thank you," was all she said to me before taking her child's hand and walking away. "What's wrong, sweetie?"

"You're welcome," I replied to her deaf ears.

I found a seat just as the show was beginning. I remember the vice-principal strutting up the steps of the stage in her blue skirt suit, determined to outdo all previous 1st grade talent show hosts. The music stopped. Some chewing and chattering continued.

"Ahem," the woman was not clearing her throat, she actually said '*ahem.'* I hate that.

"Good evening everyone, as you know, I'm Vice-Principal Keystone, and welcome to our Duman Elementary 1st grade talent show!"

There were just a few claps. She knew she needed to up her game.

"Really, truly, your children are the kindest, smartest, most wonderful children I have ever had the pleasure of working with," she spoke louder. Got the whole room applauding with that one. "I mean that from the bottom of my heart."

I looked around at the audience. They were buying this crap? Last week my boy told me the whole classroom ganged up on Jeffery, making fun of him for having long arms. He said he didn't join in, but I still wouldn't call him kind, let alone smart.

"There is so much passion and talent in all of these students. I know we're all in for a very special treat tonight."

While she was explaining the show, I saw about a third of the parents stand up and get their iPhones out to start filming. *Really*? They were going to record the entire show? I could barely sit through this once, let alone again at home.

The first kid up was John, Mike Matthews' kid. I remembered him from last year's kindergarten show when he did one single somersault, at least that's what I think he was attempting, but no one really knows what that was. We couldn't wait to see what the prodigy had in store for us this time. John waltzed up on stage, tried to pull a cartwheel—*twice*—and then took a bow. Most people didn't even know if they were supposed to clap for that or not until Tightskirt said, "Let's have a round of applause for that wonderful performance."

Mike, it's good that you don't put any pressure on

your kid to be that impressive, but please for everyone's sake, set the bar just a little higher. You could see John was way too proud of that little half-cartwheel he did.

Next was Jazmine Demarco, the singer. She walked on in a glittery wedding dress that looked like it would cost as much as my mom's health insurance, and she has diabetes. Her song started— *I Like It,* by Cardi B. The music was so loud, I could only hear Jazmine singing when she got off-key, which really was often enough. Killed the crowd, they loved it, some even started clapping to the beat near the end.

People either take this too seriously or don't care at all. I could see her lawyer dad in the corner talking on the phone the whole time. Her mother was in the front row, mouthing the lyrics and doing hand motions to her child as if that would help her remember them.

Jeffery came out next, did something with a yoyo, I think. All I remember were those ape-like arms. Brody wasn't lying.

Then a whole lot more singing and dancing, which upset me. In almost every single talent show I've ever seen in person or on TV, a singer has won. It drives me nuts. Little kids singing is not even cute for me anymore, this ruined it. If I see one more seven-year-old that thinks they can sing, I'll lose it.

Even that barbie dress girl was a part of it. I shouldn't have encouraged her. At least she looked confident enough on stage without makeup, though. I can't believe how many of those seven-year-olds wore makeup.

Thank God my son is so much more creative than all that. He actually built something for his act. I couldn't calm Brody down on the drive there. He was so nervous, shaking in his seat holding his shoebox.

"It's fine," I told him, "You'll do great, you really will."

It didn't help that we were "late," meaning we were fifteen minutes early, but still the last ones to show up. As soon as I parked the car, he didn't even say bye, he just sprinted into the building with his little legs, holding his box out in front of him.

What kind of pressure do they put on these kids?

After I had sat through an hour of that singing crap, Brody was finally up. He walked onstage with his shoebox trembling in his hands and no background music or anything. Just dead silence. He methodically opened his box and dumped out a whole bunch of Legos. A few parents laughed. The smug rich ones who knew beyond a doubt that the Beyoncé Lip Sync was going to win the talent show.

Something happened to the audience during Brody's act, though. I saw all the faces turn from amused to captivated. In less than one minute, Brody made a perfect model helicopter from fifty pieces. My kid memorized the exact steps it took to make this thing. He spent hours perfecting the process until he could do it in less than a minute. He used only the pieces he needed, and the helicopter came out looking impressively detailed.

People started clapping one by one. I saw some parents begin to look at each other with expressions of *not bad,* and *that was pretty cool.* Some still laughed. I whistled and clapped louder than all of them.

Little did we know that he wasn't done with his act yet. While the audience was still applauding, he twirled the propeller and then chucked the helicopter into the air with a big smile on his face. Most people stopped clapping then. It flew in a gigantic arc and came crashing down in front of the chairs where it exploded into fifty individual Lego pieces again. The people were stunned. All clapping stopped, all laughter stopped, everything was just silent.

"Yes!" I yelled and clapped again, alone. Then he bowed and walked off the stage before they had any time to react.

"Well, wasn't that fun," Tightskirt said and hurriedly started the next set while people were still murmuring about what had just happened. Then, while the next act was going, my son came out into the audience. No other kids did this the whole night. He picked up every one of the Legos scattered across the floor. Whenever he walked by a parent, they would whisper, "good job," to him. He just smiled at all of them.

Then something sparked in me that made me need Brody to win. Not because he was so much better than all these other kids, but to show these people that he wasn't worse. *I'm one of them,* I thought, but I couldn't help it.

Whether he won or not, at least he stood out, which is more than anyone expected of him. I remember joining his class on bring your parent to school day. I hate that day. All the other parents tried to make themselves out to be so professional, yet fun. One guy was sporting the pink, ugly bracelet his daughter made for him while still wearing the nice tie and slacks. I had a suit, too, but it didn't mean anything, not when you're the garbage man.

The kids loved the firefighter, the police officer, the doctor, and even the construction worker. None of the rest of us even had a chance. At least the lawyer was as boring as I had expected. Even his daughter lost interest and started playing games on her phone during his turn in the spotlight. Serves him right. Girl-with-no-makeup's mother wasn't bad—a journalist for National Geographic, but of course, none of the kids understood what a journalist was. Went over their heads.

When my son, this angel, introduced me to his class, he was as proud as any of the other kids were.

"My dad's a garbage collector and he's a great dad," he said. Then it was my turn to say something about my job, but how much can a guy really say about that?

All I said was, "Well, someone's gotta do it." Got a few laughs.

At the end of the night when the winner was decided, I was just as nervous as everyone else. *Show 'em, Brody.*

"And the winner is..." the vice principal said and

paused for effect, "Jazmine Demarco."

You gotta be kidding me. Cardi B girl. Her dad's eyes perked up when her name was mentioned. First time his focus was not on his phone. She came out on the stage again dancing. Applause everywhere. Her mother screamed and ran up to the stage. I could swear there were tears in her eyes.

§

There is more symmetry between the world of adults
and the world of children than we realize.

§

AUTO REPAIR SHOP

Auto Repair Shop was by no means the only auto repair shop in Toulon, Illinois, as one might mistakenly assume from its name. It was one of seven. I asked Mr. Garcia once why he named the shop what he did, and not *Garcia's Auto*, or something intuitive like that. He just laughed and said, "Because I know good business."

I admit, it had turned out to be a smart move in some ways. While the other six repair shops focused on their own specialties and had a consistent customer base, Auto Repair Shop got most of the travelers, new-in-towns, and anyone else who didn't know any better. Business was high in summer months when new people were coming through, but slow in the winter months when the only people left in town were the ones who did know better.

It wasn't a terrible mechanic shop, we were only really dishonest with about half of the customer base.

Only the ones that deserved it. Mr. Garcia was used to dealing with suckers, and didn't quite mingle well with the other types of people that came in.

There was one thing that happened that could pretty much explain what kind of person Mr. Garcia was. It was during the slow months when I was his only employee. Dead of winter, no cars in sight. I spent most of the time cleaning—sweeping and mopping the floors, scrubbing the walls and windows. It was days like those that made me want to quit, but I never did.

I was almost finished polishing all the tools, hoping he would send me home, when I heard the familiar muttering of a car entering the parking lot. Mr. Garcia's head perked up. He had been pacing the store the whole time until now, head down, hands clasped behind his back like some mastermind plotting a strategy.

"BMW," he whispered before the car was even in view.

"No way," I said.

I was hoping it was just someone looking for directions, going home had already been set in my mind, but the car pulled up in front of the garage and stopped. Sure enough, it was a grey BMW convertible, one of the old roadsters, but I couldn't tell you the exact model. I noticed immediately that the license plate said California. Mr. Garcia and I raised our eyebrows at each other. He gave a wink and marched out to meet the customer. Any time he gave that look to me, it meant he was about to show off. I always acted really interested in his sales techniques. That was why I was working now, and none of the other employees were. He liked to be appreciated. I still could not imagine that this stranger was here for service, though, not with that car.

I watched the short man get out of his fancy convertible in the foot-deep snow, wearing just a button-up shirt, slacks, and loafers. Mr. Garcia shook the man's shivering hand and led him inside. The little bell rang as they opened the door. "You're in luck," he was saying, "I happen to specialize in German automobiles, even though I am Italian."

Good thing he didn't ask for a BMW mechanic certification or anything.

Also, Pablo Garcia was Spanish, not Italian. Moved here when he was about ten and still today has a very Spanish accent. Always speaks automatically in Spanish whenever he is deep in thought or angry or making a joke. In our town, most people can't tell the difference between a Spanish and an Italian accent. I don't think they could even distinguish the two languages from one another, or foreign languages in general.

Being Italian here immediately establishes you as either a pizza chef or a car mechanic. I wish I had that luck, I'm Norwegian. People assume I'm a bank teller just by looking at me. If Garcia told them he was Spanish, people would have just ended up confusing him with Mexicans, because they speak Spanish too. That wouldn't be the best business strategy around here.

"So, what is the problem with your car, sir?" Garcia asked with the subtle superiority, and yet down-to-earth-ness that customers love so much.

"Well, itsssa, um, it's not running that well at all I think. Started about a couple days ago..."

And he went on to describe what he thought was wrong with it while I tried to keep a straight face. I could see Garcia's greedy eyes light up more and more. Soon he stopped him and said, "I can guess that starting your car is also a problem."

"Yes! How'd you know?"

"It is my job to know this," he said, with great mystery.

Even I knew what was wrong with the car. Based on what I knew about this guy, it was low on engine coolant. BMW-man obviously was not accustomed to cold weather, obviously rich, and knew nothing about the car he was driving. Probably on his way from California to Chicago, stopped at a hotel, and barely got his car started this morning in the snow without antifreeze. It wouldn't be long until the engine shut down. It was a miracle he was even here. He probably didn't even know what the words coolant or antifreeze meant. What kind of nitwit like that drives a classic BMW?

Mr. Garcia didn't even mention antifreeze, or the cold weather, or the fluids.

He started with some lines he used for every older car, "They are tricky, but simple, like a vintage wine." Then he worked his way through the engine choking up, to the pistons, to the transmission, until the customer went from trying to pretend he was following along to being clearly impatient and ready to pay for everything and get out.

I kept cleaning, almost not believing my ears. By the time I finished, Mr. Garcia had sold him—not on a fixed leak or radiator replacement—but a brand-new engine. He hadn't even looked under the hood yet. Money-For-Brains believed every word the Spaniard said.

And why shouldn't he? I caught myself asking.

"But," the dweeb said, "I'm visiting my family in Chicago for Christmas. How will I get there?"

"No, no," Garcia replied, "Engine replacement is no option." He looked at me. "It is three-day job, no?"

"Sure is," I said, probably not believably.

"There is the train station that is not far from here," he continued, "I will personally drop you off there. Come."

"Oh, thank you, really."

"Prego," the Italian hero said and motioned for me to get the paperwork.

I brought back a pen and the stack of papers on a clipboard and handed them to the man. He took the clipboard from me but pulled his own pen out of his shirt pocket. Idiot signed it all, then paid in full with his credit card. Who was this guy, Bill Gates?

"It's a lot of money, but I feel good to get her finally fixed completely."

"Guaranteed," Garcia said, "It will run no problem

when you are back." He looked at me and said, "Keep up shop."

"Guaranteed."

"Ciao," he said, and they were out the door.

"Adiós."

They drove to the train station, and I kept up shop, a.k.a., took a forty-five-minute break. My boss was looking extremely satisfied with himself when he got back.

"This is how you sell, Johnny. I hope you were paying good attention."

"Oh, I was," I said, adding extra enthusiasm to each word to make him buy it.

By the way, my name is not Johnny, it's Johann. I don't know why I'm including that detail now, but you probably won't remember, because this is the boring middle section of the story. I bet you'll forget my real name by the end.

"We'd better order that engine if we want it done by the 22nd," I said.

"Oh Johnny, you make me laugh," and he gave his little Spanish chuckle.

We fixed the coolant leak, topped off the fluids, and it ran like a race car in the snow. Then we polished off the engine so that it looked newer than it actually was, replaced a few old-looking bolts, et voilà, a brand new engine.

The next day, a large Ram pulled into our parking lot. The driver stepped down. A big, barrel-chested, white-bearded man. Maybe it was the Christmastime atmosphere affecting me, but he looked a lot like Santa Claus. That is if Santa Claus was buff and chewed tobacco and wore a biker jacket and drove a Dodge Ram. Really just the beard now that I think of it. His biceps must have been thicker than the Beamer's tires.

Then, to our bewilderment, the BMW owner plopped down with him out of the passenger side, with his nice button-up shirt and slacks, and this time a wool jacket. I doubt the man even owned a sweater or a pair of jeans. They were the oddest-looking men I have ever seen together.

Mr. Garcia hurried outside for his usual greeting, which I could tell this time was a bad idea. They were pissed. I couldn't hear what they were saying, but I could guess. Garcia talked his talk, but they only got angrier. *Shoot,* I thought, *this guy's from Chicago, of course he knows Garcia's not Italian.*

I could see the panic in Mr. Garcia's face as he hurried to show them the "new" engine under the hood. This did not impress either of them one bit. Voices were raised even louder, and Garcia started yelling, red-faced. Then Santa threw a punch at him, right on his jawbone. I could hear the collision from in the store. Shorty took a cheap shot between his legs while he was dazed, and he doubled over.

Then the real "fighting" began. Fighting is in quotation marks because it was not a fight. It was probably the most pathetic thing I've ever seen. I'm not sure he would have even won a one-on-one match with Dweeb.

'C+' for effort, though. He wasn't giving up.

I ran outside and yelled, "Hey!" But Santa turned and glared at me, daring me to join in. I hurried back inside and dialed 9-1-1.

The phone conversation went something like this:

"9-1-1, what is your—"

"This is an emergency! My boss is getting beat up in the parking lot, send an ambulance now, I don't know how much more he can take."

"All right, calm down, I need you to describe the situation for me."

"I just did!"

"We need to know how many police officers need to be dispatched as well, can you describe the situation?"

"Cops? I guess you can send them, but they're finishing up now, so they'll probably be long gone before you guys show up."

Then I knew I couldn't just stand there like an idiot anymore. I had to do something. She said something else, but I didn't hear what. I put the phone down on the counter and walked over to the glass door, viewing the carnage. At this point, Garcia's face was being shoved into the snow, probably suffocating to death. He was still squirming a lot, though, so there was hope. Santa Claus turned his huge head toward me again. I chickened out.

'C+' for Garcia, 'D–' for me.

"**H**ello? Sir, are you still there? What happened?" I

heard the woman's voice yelling through the phone.

"**A**m I supposed to do something?" I ran over and asked her.

"**N**o, do not take action. Please stay inside and describe the men and any vehicles to me."

Good, *that's what I want to hear.*

"**E**ven if it means he'll get more hurt?" I said, "Damn, well, I'll do as you say, but I'm telling him you made me stay."

"That's fine. License plates, please."

And then I had a decision to make. I could give the dispatcher the right information, and those idiots would be caught, but then they would spill everything about how Garcia scammed the moron. Auto Repair Shop would be ruined. Garcia might even get arrested when more stuff came to light. Or, I could give them the wrong information, he would lose a quart of antifreeze and his wallet, and the criminals would not be found. All this would blow over, and business would resume as usual.

I knew exactly what Mr. Garcia wanted me to do.

I did exactly the opposite, reading the license plates to both vehicles carefully and describing the pair as well as I could before they drove off. I knew I had just betrayed him, but I was really helping him, too.

Auto Repair Shop was shut down before June. Probably for the best. Garcia never asked me if I had anything to do with it, even though I always thought he would.

After the Chicago gang left, I walked out to the bleeding form of Pablo Garcia laying still in the snow. I heard him wheezing and moaning, which put me at ease.

I wasn't sure he would be alive, let alone be able to walk again, but he had enough strength left to limp back to the shop with me. He was bleeding from his lip, his eye, both nostrils, and probably most internal organs. Every inch of his body was either bruised, bleeding, or swelling. Each time he breathed in, he would cough, and each time he coughed, he cried just a little.

It might have been because of the big-gulp-sized lump on his forehead that was still growing, but he managed to let loose one of his classic Spanish chuckles and say, "No recuperan el dinero."

It's really too bad I don't speak Spanish.

§

Another delectable slice of symmetry, this book was published on 02/20/2020.

§

ARE WE WHO WE ARE

Are we who we are?
We are not, are we?
Who, not what, not who
we are not. Are we?
Are we who we are?

I know this one seems simplistic, but the symmetry is still interesting. It's the same as Life and Death as far as reading vertically or horizontally in a grid, and the same as Mirror as far as reading backwards. Start from any corner, reading in any perpendicular direction you want, and the words will always be in the same order.

are	we	who	we	are
we	are	not	are	we
who	not	what	not	who
we	are	not	are	we
are	we	who	we	are

ARMENIA

Nobody knows about Armenia now, one hundred years after it happened. I was in Yerevan, Armenia with some friends when we visited the genocide museum.

What I remember about that place, more than the hundreds of naked bodies being thrown into a trench, more than the huge lists of all the people who were raped, drowned, burned, and murdered, is a single child's face in one picture. She isn't scared or sad. She's angry. That sticks to me.

I got back to our van feeling horrible, in shock, but they were already laughing about a joke someone had just made.

NATURE MAN

I've had worse. I've had worse, I was convincing myself. *True, but I've never sprained my knee on a run by myself before.* I limped up the untrod terrain with three miles left until the gate. Not too far. My knee swelled up more after every step. *I've still had worse.* Reception here. Options: call a friend to bail me out, call 911 to bail me out, or keep going alone. I chose the only real option a man could ever choose. Limping forward wasn't a terrible nuisance to me if I stayed clear of the edge. I've always been an optimist. I got to spend more time in nature, and this would make a good story for the pals.

The knee stiffened from pain a few times when my feet slipped on loose rocks, but it wasn't unbearable if I focused on what was important. After the first mile, my right leg was so swollen that I couldn't see the kneecap anymore. It was turning blue. Every step was utter misery. I weighed my options, and of course, pressed on again. That's when I fell, a nice ten-foot drop, knee snapping, no more cell reception. *I haven't had worse.*

§

Armenia is exactly 100 words, and Nature Man is 200 words. The only other story with an intentional word count is Mercy, with 1212 words, a wonderfully symmetric number.

Another fun fact, Armenia is the only true story in this entire collection.

§

THE TUNNEL

A low, dark tunnel presented itself in front of the old man, causing an unexplainable feeling of fear. **B**ent over to see in, he was questioning whether or not he should explore it, if only for the sake of his own boldness. **C**rouching down, he decided to go forward into the mysterious hole in the rock. **D**rops of water splashed onto his neck, and he shuddered. **E**very step was drawn and calculated with his shaky legs. **F**ive minutes passed, and he had only gone a dozen yards. **G**aping blackness was all that was before him now, no more color in this world.

He stopped and screamed as a cold hand touched his arm. **I**n a frenzy of movements, he flailed about to fend off the deathly touch. **J**umping, he rapped his head on the ceiling. **K**icking, he glanced his foot off a stone. Losing balance, he slipped to his back and was too dazed to run. Mindful of every breath, his wide eyes stared ahead for whatever horror had touched him. Nothing was there, and soon he started to feel foolish. Of course nothing was there, he was in an empty cave.

Pushing fear aside, he plunged deeper into the darkness. Quality of air was growing steadily worse. Rock ahead, rock behind, rock above, rock below, he began to feel secure in the solidness around him. Suddenly, he stopped again, hearing the unmistakable whisper of his own name. Terrified, he listened for some minutes. Unbroken silence filled them, aside from the droplets falling musically to the rock floor. Volumes of horrid imaginations again poured through his mind.

"Who are you," he screamed. Xylophone tones of the water were all he heard as he stood rigid.

"You," a voice emanated from the pitch black in front of him, "I am you."

Zeal for the truth began to conquer the man, and he continued.

THE LENGTH OF A SHADOW

When Susan and Frederick conceived their first child, they weren't really in love. Neither of them wanted a baby, but they decided that it could have been a blessing to them, so they got married and bought a cheap house on the edge of town. If those first nine months were sprinkled with doubt, the next few were drenched in it. Susan gave birth to Henry on June 12, 1926. The pain of childbirth for her soon became the pain of a stayed life. She needed changes and excitement in her life, not routine. Fred's job could hardly afford all three of them, and the bills were ever-increasing.

Susan, unfortunately, had a bad sort of mental condition, her normal motherly instincts must not have been as well placed as in other women. She would have horrible thoughts, even when she tried not to.

One evening, almost a year after his son was born,

Freddy came home from work to find Henry crying in his crib, but Susan was not there to calm him. "Sue!" he yelled and strode to their bedroom when she did not answer.

She was passed out on the bed. He shook her, and she turned toward him. "Whhaa..." her drowsy voice asked, but then she heard the crying, and such a poison settled on her face.

"I'm not a fan of comin' home to this," Fred said.

She slumped off the bed.

"No one said this was gonna be easy, but it was our choice, so you gotta pull your end."

Susan kept her back turned to him and went to pick up the crying baby.

Fred wandered to the kitchen. The stove was empty, and there was a coffee spill that hadn't been cleaned up yet. "You haven't even made dinner," he said.

"Or lunch or breakfast," she finally made eye contact.

"Well maybe you can live like that, but I can't. I need food."

"Once he calms down. We need to make sacrifices, remember?" She went to the kitchen, swaying the crying baby.

"You don't think I'm making sacrifices? I work 12 hours, Susan, then I come home to this."

"You're the one who wanted to keep him."

"I ain't giving my son to an orphanage, don't bring that up again."

"I didn't bring it up."

"Why can't you just calm him down already?"

"You want to try to make it shut up?" Susan said.

Right as she said it, she slipped on the coffee spill and almost dropped her son. A look of horror came over both of their faces. The baby screamed louder. Fred just stood in a quiet anger, who knows what he would have done if she had not been holding Henry.

"I'm sorry Fred," her lip trembled.

"I'm getting out of here since you know what you're doing so well," he grabbed his coat.

Susan followed him, "Fred, wait, there's something else."

Fred walked out the door, "I'm gettin' some real food."

"I need to tell you something," she said faster, but he got in the car. "Fred, I'm pregnant again," she pleaded. He started the car. "Do you hear me!"

And he was gone.

When she finally breastfed the baby enough for it to fall asleep, she laid it down and sat for a long time. *Why did life have to become horrible as soon as our baby came,* she thought, but she felt guilty for thinking it. Then another idea slithered into her mind that should have never been there. *No,* she whispered, *I couldn't.* But still, she thought.

Enough thinking can get a person anywhere, and as she struggled to put the idea out of her head, it steadily convinced her. There was a way that she and Fred could be happy. As her mind wandered, she was able to settle her thoughts into a careful design. With no guilt or second thoughts, she crept to her baby. Without really looking at it, she picked it up and stalked out the back door into the frozen night and gently laid the baby on the ground, still wrapped in its blanket. She walked back into her house before it started crying, and then it was muffled enough for her to begin a quiet, restful sleep.

Fred usually came back a day later from his tantrums, so her plan was to go out early in the morning and warm the thing up inside before he got home, then she would cry and cry when he walked in the door. Of course, they would both be heartbroken for a season, but they would move on, and he would be much more tender with their second. She did not know, however, that someone else had seen what she had done.

* * *

There are things in this world which most humans do not understand: the feeling of love, the reality of pain, the nature of day and night. Love can elude anyone's grasp just as they start to feel it. Pain is always relative, so no one can truly understand another's hurt.

With day and night, light and darkness, humans do already understand some things. Day, they know, is light because of the yellow dwarf star that our world orbits around. Light photons travel for eight minutes before hitting Earth's surface. Night is a shadow from the sun, an absence of photons, dark. That is where human knowledge stops. But curiously, Night is not only a shadow. Night is alive, as much as any other person is. More than this, Night is a woman. Some have even seen her. They say, "She is lovely," "No, hideous." "She was blue," "No, black." She is never quite possible to explain. Would Night be a harsh cold or a cool relief from the day? A wicked queen of bats and wolves, or the gentle bringer of stillness and dreams? One can only guess until one meets her face to face, as Susan Miller has.

Night was watching Susan, as she had watched so many other things in the shadow of the world, too many tragedies. Who knows what made this one different, or whether it was by pity or anger, but the woman glided closer. The baby was crying hard, not many tears, just screaming as loud as it could. *How could the mother let this happen?* The baby's eyes opened. They were as green as leaves in the moonlight, staring into the dark, begging to live. This made the woman want more than anything to help, but she was not completely sure how. She reached her fingers out to the baby's lips.

"Please stop crying," she said, and it lessened. She brought the infant up to her shoulder and embraced it like it was her own. Swaying, she began to sing to it a lullaby. Hesitantly at the start, like the first few drops of rain, or the first crickets to sound in the evening, but her song grew to a melody so wonderful that all the night animals became silent to listen. Her voice twisted and turned in company with the wind bending the trees around them, and the baby was lulled to sleep. Night whispered, "I give you my blessing," and kissed its tiny forehead. "You are now a part of me."

The spot that her lips touched became shaded, almost black. Then the darkened area began to spread through the infant's veins. His shivering stopped, and she could feel his warm, soft breathing on her chest. A new problem came to this heroine then. She had nowhere to put the child, but back inside the mother's house. She hated the idea of placing the child in this witch's clasp, so before she left the baby alone, she visited the mother.

Susan awoke shortly after midnight to see a woman standing at the edge of her bed. She gasped and struggled but was unable to move away, with an enormous pressure on her chest.

"You, a sin among mothers, have created this tragedy," Night said in a thin, airy voice. "Look at your son."

Susan turned her shocked face to see her son lying next to her. His skin was dark blue in the moonlight.

"See what you have done to him, for this I curse you." The room turned terribly cold. Susan could barely breathe. "You will never hurt this child again," the fragile voice continued, "When you have raised him, and he leaves you, you will end your own life."

Night exited through the paned window, but the room kept its frigidity.

When Susan could move, she grasped her baby. He was breathing. She sighed a sigh of relief so great, that it woke the exhausted infant, but he did not cry. The two of them lay there motionless until the sun rose.

* * *

When Fred rushed into the hospital room, he couldn't believe his sight. Henry didn't look alive, didn't even look real. Susan never told her husband what she had done, but neither she, Frederick, nor the doctors knew what was happening to their baby. They said it was most likely some rare type of anemia that hadn't been formally studied yet. After all the commotion, their terror was renewed when they left the hospital and found that Henry had no real shadow. That ended any hope they had of fixing Henry's condition.

They settled for, "It was meant to be," and tried to have normal lives, which was all Susan seemed to want now. Their second child they named Alexander. Frederick praised God that he never developed Henry's condition. As Henry grew, often they were afraid that he was hurting from his condition, but he acted the same as any other boy would have. All anyone knew was that he somehow had no shadow, and his skin was gray. Even more surprising than the color, though, was the lack of any. His skin looked pale and faded. Henry could walk outside on a summer day, and still appear like he was in a room with the shutters down. It was as if light itself wanted nothing to do with him.

They didn't want him in school at first—for not all unselfish reasons—but Henry and Alex insisted on going together. They thought that it couldn't hurt him too much, with Alex there to protect him. Alex was more like the older brother, Frederick always said.

Until he got to school, Henry did not fully realize that his appearance was so irregular. He had seen pictures of people in the newspaper, and they didn't look too different from him with their colorless eyes and grey skin. He thought his family members were the oddly colored ones, compared to the rest of the world in the black and white paper. How odd this must have seemed to him when he saw real other children besides his brother. Everyone was all white or tan or brown, and everyone had a weird black thing that followed them around everywhere. But he only had himself and no black thing to sit next to him when no one else did. Alex did his best to convince the other kids that Henry really wouldn't hurt them and that he wasn't a ghost, but no one believed him. Even teachers were solemnly off-put by the child.

Henry decided to cover himself with a bedsheet when he went to school on the second day. His mother told him not to, but he cried and convinced her to let him. It didn't make anyone stare at him less, but during lunch, a 3rd grader was brave enough to touch his covered arm. To his delight, this broke the no-touch barrier that the other kids had against him. But then the touches turned into pushes and trips and slaps and punches. By the time the sheet made it home, it was ripped, muddy, and blood stained. The next day he left it at home, and most of the kids were too scared to touch him again. His blood, they found out, was almost pure black.

The insults were almost always worse, however. "My name's Henry," he would keep reminding everyone, but they still called him Ghost, Freak, or Satan. It seemed to Henry that his skin wasn't the only reason people were mean or scared of him, maybe it really was his soul.

For the first few years, Henry's only friend was Alex, while Alex soon developed friends of his own. Maybe it was because of the peer pressure, or maybe because of his father's example, but Alex started spending less time with Henry as they grew older. Who could blame Alex? Henry did not seem dependent on his younger brother, and he was too good at pretending to enjoy solitude. Henry learned the art of hiding pain. He never complained about his condition, and he never said, "I hate myself," aloud.

He grew to enjoy some parts of his abnormality. In shadows, especially at night, he was barely visible. Sometimes he could sneak right in front of people, and they would not know he was there. As he grew, he learned that he was very good at thieving. There were a few older kids at school, delinquents and riff-raff, who were overly delighted with this. He would steal pocket watches, rings, change, or anything else loosely connected for them. His new friends were amazed at how stealthily he could glide next to people in the shadows. Usually, there was a shout or jump as people felt a finger touch them, but they wouldn't see anything, so they would just keep walking a little faster. The friends thought this was hilarious. Henry usually didn't want the things he was stealing, but he was at least good at something, and he at least had people who wanted him around.

Of course, he'd have terrible thoughts, but some nights, when it was too much for him, a comforting, familiar presence would come into his room, which would last until morning. Sometimes he even saw a woman floating at the edge of his bed. Whenever he did, she would talk or sing to him. They conversed about school, trees, people, and anything else Henry liked to talk about. He would always look forward to these nights, and he began to have a hard time sleeping if the woman did not come. One night, Henry asked, "Lady, who are you?"

"I told you before, child, I am Night," her wafting voice sounded like air.

"But you look like a person."

"And so do you," Night laughed.

"Why do you always come to my room?"

"Because I love you, and I have been watching you since your birth."

"Really? My birth, was I always like this?"

"No, once you were just like the other humans."

"Then how was I cursed, do you know?"

"You think you are cursed?"

"Yes, I hate looking like I do."

"You are not cursed, child."

"But that's what they all tell me."

"You do not have to listen to them. They are wrong. It is your mother's fault either way."

"It is? No, Mum would never harm me."

"No, she will not ever again, and you can stay with her until you no longer want to. But believe me, child, she did harm to you, and she will pay for it," while she was saying this, Night started to appear much more frightening, and the confused boy hid under his covers. Night kissed the sheets and left.

Henry told his mother about it the next day, and her face paled. "Henry, that's crazy! A woman coming to your room at night. And accusing me of d-doing this to you! Don't tell your father, Henry. He wouldn't like it."

However, Frederick did find out that something was going on at night. He woke up sometimes to hear voices coming from inside the house, so he would burst all the doors open, but find nothing ever out of place. The kids would be sound asleep in their beds— actually Henry was awake some of the times. That worried Fredrick: either there were intruders in his house, or Henry was talking to spirits, and he greatly preferred the first option. He wasn't going to raise ghost talkers in this house.

Henry and Alex were surprised one evening to see their father walk in with a revolver. "Now I'm ready for any intruders comin' in here," he said, but later he locked the gun in the basement and said, "I don't want ya lookin' at that gun. You look at a gun 'n pretty soon you want to use it, and I ain't raisin' criminals in this house."

* * *

One day, Henry came home before Alex. He wanted to surprise his parents and show them that he could be good too. Just before he opened the door, he heard a piercing scream come from inside. It sounded like Mother. Henry ran through the house to his parents' bedroom. There was blood on the floor. Susan was lying face up on the ground, still alive. Henry had come just in time. He screamed for help, and she lifted her terrified face to see him.

"Henry!" She said out of breath, and too weak to cry, "go get bandages, and call the hospital."

He ran for the medicine drawer as fast as he could, and called the hospital, telling them that his mother had been attacked. "Mum," he said, "is the person still here?"

"No," she faintly said, "don't worry, you're safe."

The ambulance arrived shortly and took Susan and Henry to the hospital. There was, unfortunately, no way of contacting Fred at work, so they left a note at home. He arrived in his car with Alex, in a frenzied rush. Poor Alex had seen the note and had to wait another hour for their dad to get home and take him. She had just woken up by the time they got in. Fred was so relieved to see her alive, but after seeing the two bandages on only her wrists, his expression changed to fear, anger even. This confused Henry. Why would he not be happy that the invader only hurt her wrists, and not more of her? The person did not even steal anything. He must not have had time when he heard the door open.

"My darlings," she said when she saw them and put her shivering hands out.

Henry and Alex gently embraced her, careful to avoid touching her wrists. Fred stood and waited his turn. It seemed like Susan was trying to say something to her husband, but she wasn't getting the words out. She finally whispered, "sorry," to him when her children were farther away.

She had to stay a lot longer than Henry thought she would have. The police came and talked to her, but he couldn't stay in the room for that. They just asked her some questions, she said. A specialty doctor also came in to see her and ask her things. Alex and Henry couldn't agree on what his purpose was. Finally, this specialty doctor allowed her to go home. Apparently, he was in charge of healing Mother now.

Their home was different after this, but not at all how Henry had expected. He thought his father would take the gun into their bedroom to prevent further attackers, but it stayed locked in the basement. They had to take out the locks to every room before Susan got home. Henry thought this was ridiculous; why would they only make it easier for an intruder? It was the doctor who made the decision, Henry knew, but he didn't know why his dad did everything the man said. Frederick only kept the lock on the basement.

* * *

After that Henry made it through most of school without stealing. He didn't have much trouble, his old buddies all dropped out before he did, but he was coming home after school one day when he heard his name called. His head jerked up; people rarely used his real name.

It was Leroy and Arthur. They ran up to him and said, "Where you been off to? Heard you died."

"Hey fellas, sorry I've been doing school."

Leroy laughed, "School ain't oughtta take that much time, 'sides y'always hated it."

"I've been trying to take care of my mum."

"Your mam hah? Henry, you're our brother, we don't like to hear that y'only lookin' out for mam, and not for us," Leroy said. Arthur just grinned.

"I'm sorry guys."

"Well I'll tell ya, Henry, it's been real hard without ya."

Henry caught a glimpse of a large woman wearing a fur coat walking behind them.

Leroy's eyes followed his, and he smiled, "how 'bout just one more, for old times' sake?"

"I don't really want to steal for you."

"Why not? Nothin stopped ya before."

"Well, I'm not a criminal anymore."

"Ya think we're criminals? Ya think y'any better than us because ya got a dad who makes money?"

"He doesn't make that much, and I don't think I'm better than you, really."

"Ha, sure sounds like that. Well, tell ya what, you steal that purse from high lady over there, and you can keep it all."

"I can't," Henry said with clear regret in his voice.

They shook their heads, "Wow, you really can't, ya pansy."

"I ain't a pansy."

"Na, I think you are, it would explain a lot," they inched away from him.

"Guys, wait."

They took some steps back. "We don't want nothin' to do with pansies, Henry."

His own name caught him off guard again. "No, I'll do it," he admitted.

"She's gettin' away."

Henry hurried to the large, rich woman, and waited until she walked under a shadow, then disappeared under it. It was only then that he saw she wasn't wearing a purse. He felt that he had to leave with something, so he grabbed the fur coat. The woman screamed and thrashed behind her, but when she saw only a dark blur, her face turned to horror. "Ghost! Demon!" she yelled.

She fumbled out of the coat and sprinted away, but

a few steps later stumbled in her high heels and hit her head. Henry stared at her, but she wasn't moving.

When he looked back at his friends, they were already running away, laughing. Henry left but came back to see if she was all right. She was gone, so he prayed that she wasn't dead.

He realized that her coat was still in his hands. He thought about throwing it in a mud puddle, and thought about leaving it there, but decided to keep it.

By the time he got home, Alex was standing outside. "Henry, what are you doing? Where'd you get that?"

"I just found it," Henry said.

"Well, you shouldn't bring it inside."

"Why not? I think Mum will like it."

"Where would you find a coat like that?"

"I found it, I told you."

"Henry, what will Dad think?"

Shrugging, he said, "Mom'll look pretty."

Alex shook his head, "I'm only trying to look out for ya. I don't want Dad to be mad at you."

"I'll tell you when I need your help, Alex."

"Fine."

Susan was also cautious about the coat initially, but at seeing Henry's regretful face, she put it on and said she was thrilled with the texture. Fred came home while she had it on, and smiled, "Wow, you look lovely," he said.

She blushed in front of them and said, "thank you."

"Where did you get it?"

She paused, "Mrs. Locksley gave it to me, she had

just got another one."

"That's nice. We'll have to thank them somehow."

"Oh, I'll figure something out, don't worry about it," Susan said.

Three days later, when Henry had disappeared after class, Alex was strolling home. His feet stopped at their porch. The daily paper was lying there. Near the bottom of the roll was a photograph of a fur coat. Alex snatched it up and tore off the rubber band. It was the coat, exactly like the one Henry brought home. He didn't even need to read the caption:

```
STOLEN RARE COAT, REPORT IF SEEN
          $50 REWARD
```

He ran to the fireplace, where a log had been smoldering, and threw it in, but the rolled-up paper bounced off the log into the ash. He thought about pushing it into the coals, but he stopped and walked away, leaving it unsinged.

* * *

Henry came home to hear his mother screaming. His dad's car was here this time. He ran in and saw Alex sitting on the floor with his head between his legs.

Alex's bruised face shot up, "No stop," he warned as Henry rushed past him into their parents' bedroom.

"No, no," Susan screamed, "it wasn't him!"

"Don't you lie to me!" Fred screamed back.

Henry came in to see that his mother had a bloody lip. He tensed his muscles. The fur coat was in his father's hand. Fredrick glared at Henry with an intensity that he had rarely witnessed.

Susan was whimpering, "I stole it, not Henry."

Fred was about to hit her again.

"I took it," Henry blurted out.

"Finally manned up, huh?" Fred said, "Think this makes you tough? You think you gonna get away with this?"

Alex walked in. "Dad," was all he could say.

"You leave this room right now, Alex," Fred pointed at him, eyes still on Henry "Henry don't need you anymore, don't need any of us, do you?"

"Fred, he's your son," Susan pleaded.

Fred shook his head and stormed out down the hallway. "Alex, keep him in here."

They heard the telephone being dialed, then Fred's voice said, "Yes, I need the police."

"No!" Susan screamed and scrambled out of the bedroom.

Henry and Alex stared at each other, then Alex stepped out of his way.

"Yes, I have him and the coat right now," Fred stated, but then heard the front door open. He went outside and called, "Henry, come back right now. I know you're hiding here. You will pay for this!"

Susan ran out, "Henry please don't hide. We'll work it out. Don't be scared of us!"

But Henry wasn't hiding, and he wasn't scared. He was heartbroken and running. He was running and running, he had never sprinted such a long distance before. He tripped into some lovers walking on the street but kept going. He could hear the woman's all too familiar shriek as she laid eyes on what had pushed her. Only when he reached the highway did he stop, gasping on his back. Night found him crying there.

"Child," she descended and took on her human form.

"My parents don't want me," Henry cried.

"That may be true," she said, "but they do not deserve you." Henry didn't argue. She continued, "I knew this day would come, yet I cannot tell the future, but humanity never changes."

"I don't care. I'm lost, I have nothing."

"You have your life. Be thankful for that."

He gave a slight nod but kept sobbing.

"If you would like, I can take you anywhere you want to go."

"Right now?"

"Yes."

Henry looked at the stars and gave a sigh, "How about up there?"

If Night's face was capable of lighting up, it would have. "It is possible if you wish it."

"Really," Henry said, "You're serious?" He thought about it, then said, "I would like nothing better."

He had never seen Night so proud of herself. "I can go as far as the moon. But you will not be able to breathe there. It is freezing, and there is no water or food."

"How will I survive?"

"I will make you like I am. I can do this, but only because I trust you as my own son. I have given this power to others before, but it was abused."

"Yes!" was all Henry could say in his excitement.

Night floated off the ground above Henry and spread out her arms, and something that looked like long black curtains emerged from them, sinking onto him, dripping like molasses. He felt his shoulders and back become absorbed by the strange substance. It only hurt for a few moments, and then she started to pull him up. The sensation was frightening, he had never been off the ground before, but they kept rising. The higher they rose, the more comfortable he felt in Night's presence. He stopped being afraid of the height and enjoyed the roads and buildings becoming smaller and smaller, and landscapes opening up to a dark red horizon.

"The moon is a great distance to you, but to me, it is only the length of a shadow from here, nothing more," she explained as they floated up. "The earth casts a shadow upon the moon, which is why we can see only a portion of it now. I can ride this shadow as fast as light pushes the darkness, but you cannot travel as fast, even as you are. It would only take me just over one single second to reach it, but I will not push your body this far."

Then Night shot off. Henry felt nauseated from the

sudden momentum, and the pressure made his eyes want to pop out of his skull, but he soon adjusted. He felt almost as part of the air, and then suddenly he didn't feel anything at all, but they were still moving. He saw the full shapes of continents emerge, and then get smaller. There was barely any visible light on the earth now.

"Where are all the cities and lights?" He asked, confused.

"They are too small to see now," Night said.

Henry was astonished, and dazed, as one gets when they are unsure whether or not they are dreaming. He looked around at the infinite expanse of stars, then back to Earth. It was a full, blue and white ball. The only concept of speed he had was how fast the Earth was shrinking. The bliss and wonder of this moment went by too fast for him. Before Henry knew it, they were slowing to a stop on the new ground of the moon. Panic gripped him as he felt exposed and cold and out of breath, but soon, that faded too. There was no longer cold or warm, and there was no longer oxygen. He took a single step and glided, to his astonishment, a full ten feet. He lost his balance and fell over. Laughing, he leaped another twenty feet.

"What is this?" he asked Night but was surprised that no sound came out of his mouth.

She responded in his mind, "It is because this moon's pull is one-sixth of Earth's, and also you now have less mass because of your transformation."

"Transformation?" he looked at himself, and his

heart jumped. He was even blacker than before, and more translucent, like an actual shadow. It scared him, but the new movement kept his excitement going. A smile unbefitting of his age crept onto his lips. He crouched down, then shot up as high as he could. Some craters in the moon came into view as he went higher. He must have been hundreds of feet off the ground before he slowly fell back down.

They flew and explored for miles before Night said, "The time is nearing when I must return. Earth's shadow is almost past us, and I must continue my circuit before then."

Henry looked at Earth and saw the light of the sun peeking around the edge. He was surprised at how small the world was. It looked smaller than the moon did from Earth. "I thought the moon was smaller than Earth," he said.

"You of all people know that things do not have to be as they appear," she said, "It is an illusion that your vision tells you. Just like you. You have a soul, a heart, emotions just like any other human, but the others did not agree because of what they saw."

Henry tilted his head upward, "Some of them did."

"You mean your family."

"At least Alex and Mother."

Night looked angered at this, "You still call her that? After she abandoned you again?"

"I ran away from her, not the other way around," but then with fear, he said, "and what do you mean again?"

Night told him, "Years ago, I was traveling my circuit around the Earth like I always do, when I saw in a house a woman sitting alone with a sleeping child. I felt that I needed to stay; there was something strange about this woman's manner, and my instincts were correct. She rose and took her child outside, then left it to die lying on the cold ground and went to sleep in her house. I was not very surprised that this had happened, many worse horrors have happened at my watch, but I was still moved to help this poor creature. I touched the baby with my lips and caused what you now call a curse, but it was this that kept you alive."

"That wasn't me! My mother would never do that to me," Henry said and glided away from her.

Instead of refuting him, Night stood still and sang. Henry stopped. This melody was so familiar, but he couldn't remember where he heard it before. It seemed to draw him in, and his agitated nerves started to calm. He moved closer to Night, and it grew even more enticing. He knew this melody as he knew himself. Soon he couldn't deny it anymore and leaped into the cloud of her dress, enveloping him, folding over him.

"Now you see," she said, "I am your mother, your home. I am the one who will never abandon you."

"I know," Henry started crying, "How could she do that? And only to me, not Alex."

"The cruelty of humans disgusts me. Do not worry, she is paying for what she did."

"What?"

"I have cursed her. She raised you with guilt and

fear and regret, knowing that as soon as you left her, she would die."

"She's going to die?"

"Yes, and by her own hand. I can also kill the others who harmed you, would you like that as well?"

"What? No!" he pushed himself away from Night, "Why would you even think about killing them? Why would you make Mum do that?"

"They all deserve it."

Henry moved farther away, but when he reached the rays of sunlight, it burned his skin, and he flinched back into the darkness.

"Stop, Child. Your skin can no longer tolerate the light," Night said.

"But I was fine before," whimpered Henry.

"You are much less human now."

"No, this isn't what I wanted! None of this was what I wanted. Please, change me back."

Night spoke like she could not believe her words, "You want to be like them again?"

"I can't live like this, take me back. We can still save Mother!"

"Never speak of that woman again! You will forget her. I will make sure of it," Night looked horrendously angry. "I have given you everything. My life, love, justice, how can you not be grateful?"

"Please take me back," Henry begged.

"No. I will not let you be ruined by humans anymore, and I do not even have the ability to change you back. You must stay here and be happy with me."

She started to lift off the ground. "I will return during the next cycle. When you have grown enough, I may teach you how to visit earth again."

"No!" He jumped, grabbing her dress. She forced him off of her and rose higher. "Wait," Henry pleaded.

She looked away from him, then disappeared.

* * *

Alex crunched his feet through the fallen leaves. *Why did Henry have to do that?* It was Henry's fault after all, but Alex still felt a knot of guilt in his stomach. It had been over a day since his brother left, and he still hadn't come back. Alex knew he probably wouldn't this time. Father went too far. Still, Alex felt obligated to investigate Henry's condition. He knew everyone already had before, but he had to try. He was coming back from reading medical disorder books at the library all day again, but they wouldn't let him take any of them home. There seemed to him to be a glimmer of hope for Henry, and the only reason he left his furious study was that he realized he hadn't eaten in eight hours and headed home for supper. He wondered if he should let Henry know what he'd been doing. There wasn't a chance to right now anyway, no one knew where his brother was. No one even cared to look, not that it would have done any good.

"Dad's probably glad he's gone," Alex spouted to himself, *but what about Mum?* With her illness, there was no telling what reaction she would have. He picked up his pace. *No, she wouldn't.* Questions raged in his mind. He got home, noticing the fireplace had only ash left. Mother always kept the fire up.

"Mother? Mum," he called. Everything was quiet.

Panicked, he ran to the bedrooms, then the bathroom, "Mum, please answer."

He ran to the backyard. She was sometimes gardening, but she wasn't there either. Maybe she went out for a walk, but he knew she hated Autumn weather. *Where else could she be?* He checked every room besides the basement since it was always locked, but then it was the only place that he had not checked. He rushed to the basement to find the door wide open. The lock was broken, still hanging there.

"Mum!" he called, but only more silence answered.

*   *   *

The night sky was beautiful from where Henry stood, but he was still only looking at the earth. He felt betrayed. The earth seemed so peaceful, so harmless from up here. The loneliness he had felt his whole life was boiling up to his mind now. He was completely cut off from everything. If there was any way to get back, any sacrifice he could make, he would take it. All his life he had this small hope of being normal and having a loving family, but it was gone now. He looked at his arm. It was black, and he could see through it. The arm's outline seemed to grow and depress with his breathing. He didn't even know why he was breathing, he didn't need to anymore. It was a habit, he supposed. Putting a hand over his chest, he held his breath and listened. There was a faint pulse, at least that hadn't changed.

He realized that he couldn't feel his feet, and he looked down, but couldn't see them anywhere. Terrified, he jumped and saw them being pulled up out of the darkness. It looked like they had been spread out on the ground like cold molasses on the floor. He saw the dark swell up into his legs and become feet again. *What is happening to me?*

"Night!" he shouted but was somewhat relieved when she did not come.

He glided back down and felt his feet touch the ground. He stared at them, making sure they did not disappear this time. While he was focusing on his feet, the sun's light caught up to him, and he screamed and jumped out of the way. This time it almost felt like he teleported. In a few seconds, he must have been a thousand feet away, but it hardly felt like he had moved at all. Then he thought: *If I am like Night now, then I should be able to move like her too*, and he tried to calm down a little. Focusing on keeping his body whole, he moved into the darkness as fast as he could and shot another few thousand feet to his left. *It worked!* A shred of hope filled his spirit as he looked toward Earth again. He jumped straight up as far as he could, then looked below him and saw the slight curve of the moon's horizon. Eventually, he sank backward. He figured out that he could control how fast he dropped, also, and rushed down to the moon again. He repeated the same process, getting a little higher each time, but Earth did not look any closer, even at the highest point. *At this rate, I'll never get home.*

"I can ride this shadow as fast as light pushes the darkness," he remembered Night saying. *How does she do that?*

He concentrated and closed his eyes, and with caution, imagined his body blending in with his surroundings. He felt connected to the whole shadow now, but he could still distinguish himself from it. Opening his eyes, he could not see himself at all. He imagined himself floating above the ground, and was amazed when he looked down to see that the ground was fifteen feet below him.

"I'm flying," he said, and then shouted, "I'm flying!"

He started moving to the left, then up higher, and laughed in the bliss of the moment. He looked at a large grey mountain about a mile to the north of him and flew to it in less than a minute. It was still not as fast as when he was with Night, but it was something. The sun's threatening light was still steadily approaching. He was running out of time. *Just one shadow away,* he remembered and looked again at a mountain much farther away. He imagined himself being pulled there by the retreating shadow, and when he opened his eyes, his surroundings were completely different. He could see that the stream of light looked a lot farther away now, and he was on a mountain larger than the last one.

Hope flooded him again like it hadn't since he was a child. He looked longingly to Earth. He had to get back. Keeping his eyes focused on the distant sphere, he lifted himself from the ground and imagined being pulled there. He was launched faster than any of the times before. Earth was getting larger as he went. The fear of falling did not fully hit him until he neared the earth and realized he couldn't stop. He hit the atmosphere, and it hurt, but when he thought he would contact the ground, he slowed down instead of impacted. His eyes stung, and then he realized he was underwater and floated up to the surface. He laid still in the ocean water for a while, in an utter wonder of what he had just accomplished. Then the thought came to him, *I don't know where home is.* He floated higher, but all he could see or hear was water.

* * *

Alex sat in the dark outside of his house, and couldn't bear to walk in. Father was still talking to police in the basement where Mother and the revolver were both missing. *Where had she gone?* He steadily felt the anxiety increase in his veins, though he was initially relieved when he did not find her there. He called the police and searched all over the farms and streets by their house. No one he talked to had seen her.

He was standing there staring down the street when Fred and the bulls finally came out.

"Alex, ya comin' in?" Fred yelled.

Alex tore his gaze from the road and paced inside.

"It's chilly here, we gotta get a fire goin'," Fred grabbed some logs.

"Shouldn't we be searching?"

"I'm too tired. There's nothing more we can do tonight, Al. I'll skip work and we'll go tomorrow."

"But Dad, she's out there."

"I don't want to think about what she's doin' out 'ere with my gun, but whatever it is, she don't want to be found. If she did someone woulda seen her."

"I can't sleep tonight, not when she's not here."

Frederick gazed at his son, then said, "fine," and grabbed the lantern and strode out the back door.

"You don't want to search towards town?"

"Like I said, someone woulda seen 'er."

The two searched all night without luck. Exhausted at 5:00 AM, Alex nearly fainted rather than fell asleep in his bed. Fred called in, and his boss said he'd give him one day off to look for his wife. He brewed another pot.

Two days later, Fred had gotten about an hour of sleep before Alex came in and woke him, saying the police were here and wanted to speak with him. He slumped out of the room to see two men in blue standing at the door. No words can express the huge duality of emotions that this sight brought Alex and

Fred: an untamable hope of good news, and an undeniable dread of bad news. When they heard that they had found her dead body, Alex ran outside sobbing, but Fredrick stood still. He knew it would be appropriate to cry in this situation, but he didn't.

She was found at the bottom of a cliff, neck broken. The revolver was laying a few paces away from her, all the bullets fired.

"We think she must have been running from wolves or maybe a bear. We'll find it soon for sure, 'specially if she shot something," the officer was saying, but it got difficult for Fred to hear them.

"What about witnesses?" Fred interrupted them.

"Well, one woman said she'd seen a lady runnin' in her nightgown into the woods. Said she was bein' chased by the dark."

"The what?"

"Well y'see it was old lady Farnoaks who said it, and you know 'er eyesight ain't nothin' great. She said there was some big shadow chasin' after her, which is why we're thinkin' bear."

* * *

Night viewed Henry from above while he scoured a beach for signs of people. It had only been five nights since she had left him on the moon. When she could not find him there, she grew worried. Now that she saw the boy, she contemplated bringing him back there with her but decided to wait to do that. Henry had just spotted lights in the distance when she came down next to him.

"What do you want?" Henry asked with disdain as soon as he noticed her.

"I have come to take you back home," she said.

"I don't want to go with you."

"Child, please listen to me. You cannot fight against me, just make peace with me and be content."

Henry started for the lights. "I'm finding my mother."

"You will not find her," she said, and Henry looked at her, terrified. "She is dead."

Henry went still.

Night moved toward him.

"Don't touch me!" he screamed.

She quickly grabbed his arm and moved pulled him somewhere.

"Let go of me," Henry yelled, then realized that they were near his house.

"I will not approach you again, if that is your wish," Night said, "but you should know this before I leave you. Of all the curses and blessings I have given humans, none have ever been annulled until the one I gave your mother. She was not trying to end her life."

Henry wanted to ask her more, but she vanished into the air.

* * *

It's been three days, we're okay, thought Alex. He was occupied with getting ready for the University, and Fred took up double shifts at the machine shop. It seemed to be the only way that men knew how to get past grief. Alex asked Frederick to let him work at the shop with him, but he only said, "Ain't the kinda life for you."

Alex left the library at four, in time to run home and start supper. The fog was thick today, and dusk came a bit early. Fred got back later than usual, and they ate in silence. Alex knew the stew was bad, but Fred didn't mention it. He only had one bowl instead of two. Their dinner was interrupted by a voice shouting, "Let go of me." Alex looked at his father.

Fred didn't seem to hear, and he walked to his room when he was done. "I'm gonna sleep," he said to Alex.

"Okay," Alex complied.

He was curious to see who shouted, so he looked around after washing the dishes outside. Alex heard steps farther to his left.

He looked but didn't see anything. His heart rate accelerated. "Hello?" he said, "anybody there?" He walked over to where he heard the noise.

"Hi Alex," Henry said.

"Henry! Where are you?" Alex felt something touch his arm and jerked away.

"Sorry, I'm right here."

Alex continued to feel around and look past Henry.

"Alex, stop playing around," Henry said.

"I'm not playing around. Where are you?" Alex said, still groping towards him.

"You really can't see me?" Henry grabbed his brother's hand.

Alex stared down, "I can see my own hand just fine."

It wasn't until they walked well into the light from the window that Alex saw Henry completely. Like an outline in the air, no real color.

"Henry, what happened?" Alex asked.

"I... you wouldn't believe me."

"*I* wouldn't believe you? Just tell me, Hen."

"All right, there's a lady who calls herself Night. She took me to the moon and made me like this. Sunlight stings me now, too."

"Uh okay," Alex walked inside, but Henry hesitated. "He's out like a rock, don't worry."

Henry stepped in and breathed a sigh of relief when he heard his father snoring.

"I," Alex started, but waited a while to continue, "I need to tell you something."

"Is it Mother?" Henry asked. Alex nodded. "Then I know."

Alex nodded again.

"You found her?"

"Someone found her. We had a funeral yesterday."

Henry started to sob, "It's my fault."

"No, it's not!" Alex said, "she was running from a bear."

"Really?"

"Yeah, there weren't many tracks, but they don't know what else it could have been."

They cried for a bit, then Henry said, "I don't think I can stay here."

"Hen, it's fine. We'll talk to Dad tomorrow."

"I don't know if I can talk to him."

"Are you serious? Hen, you have to. We have to stick together now."

"Fine, I'll try to talk to him tomorrow," he said, "but I don't think it will end well."

Henry laid on Alex's floor all night, staring at the dark ceiling. Before he knew he had even fallen asleep, a thumping on the door woke both of them up. It was early, still dark out.

"Alex, you going to church?"

"Yes sir," Alex lit a lantern and fumbled into some nice clothes.

"You still in bed?" Fred said, and he opened the door to see Henry on the floor. No one moved. "What're you doing here?"

"I was just gonna stay for one night," Henry said.

"That doesn't answer the question."

"We thought," Alex started, but a cold glare from Fred shut him up.

"Did you want," said Fredrick, "to be welcomed back here?"

"Dad, I'm sorry."

"It's too late for an apology," said Fred, "you've ruined enough lives here."

"He hasn't ruined anyone's life!" Alex defended, but

Henry stood up and walked past his father out the door.

"Happy now? You're the one ruining lives," said Alex as he followed Henry, but the comment was unnecessary, tears were already in his dad's eyes.

Henry was in the air when Alex got outside. He shouted, but Henry kept moving, so he ran as fast as he could in the same direction. Soon a line of trees blocked his path, but he kept moving. After a while, he stopped and looked around, recognizing the area that the police led him and his dad to. He walked over to the hidden cliff and stood there, gazing down. Before he realized it, his footing slipped, and he fell. He knew he was about to die like his mother, but he landed on a spongy material instead of the ground. The air was knocked out of him, and he started to lose consciousness.

"Hey," his brother slapped him, "can you get off?"

Alex struggled and finally caught a breath. He rolled over and touched his bleeding head. "You saved me. I would have died."

"I know," said Henry.

"You saved me!"

"So what, you think it means anything?"

Alex sat up and moaned, holding his head. He turned over and puked, and then started to cry. "This is where it happened," he said. "I can't believe she's gone."

Henry could not believe it either.

"Say something, Hen, how have you said nothing

about her since you've been back?"

"I guess I can't yet," he said. "Are you all right?" referring to Alex's head.

"She was our Mum," Alex said, "I'm not doing great," meaning his heart.

The dawn sunshine started to break through, and Henry moved to the shade. "She was always close to you," he said.

"Hen, it wasn't your fault."

Henry gritted his teeth, "I know whose fault it was, but it doesn't matter. I can't stay here anyway. Dad's right about me needing to leave."

"Wait, no."

"Dad's not always wrong."

"Henry you're not a bad influence, look, you just saved my life. We'll tell that to Dad."

"It's not about Dad, it's about me. I hurt people, it always happens."

"No, you don't."

"I've always brought you down. You know it's true. We've never even been a family because of me."

"Of course we're a family."

"Well then I don't feel like a part of it," Henry continued before Alex could respond, "I know Mum tried, but I don't think she loved me deep down. And Fred always blamed me for everything."

"Hen, that's not true."

"Alex, you have to accept this. I don't belong with you. You have to move on and try to live a normal life. You're the only one who can. Mum was stuck, Fred's stuck, I am definitely stuck, but you actually have hope."

"But we have to stick together, now especially."

"No, you need to get out and live a real life."

"But families help each other."

Henry lost his temper. "You can't help me!" he yelled.

They were silent. Clouds moved in, obscuring the sun, and he was able to leave the shade and help Alex limp back to the house. Fred wasn't there when they arrived.

Alex packed his suitcase, then finally said, "All right, I'm leaving to the University tomorrow, and I'll probably find work, too."

Henry nodded.

"Where will you stay?" asked Alex.

"Probably Murphmill."

"Ha, people are definitely going to think you're a ghost, now."

They laughed.

"You think Dad will be ok?" Alex asked.

"You tell me."

"He'll be fine. We don't see much of each other anyway."

They stood there for a while. Henry finally said, "Take care of yourself," and flew southwest. He arrived at his location in a few minutes. Murphmill was the old Murphy Windmill that had been abandoned three years back. People said it was haunted, which was why it was one of the only places Henry could be alone for a while. He intended to stay there a few days and plan a way to somehow make a living in the city.

* * *

Alex found the mill two months later, but it was not deserted. A few kids were surrounding the windmill, creeping near it slowly. Henry must not be here, Alex thought.

One of the boys held up his hand for them to stop, and they all looked at him.

"I saw it move!" he whispered.

"Come on," another said, and they all continued inching forward. The one closest to the steps stopped when he reached them. Everyone else goaded him to go in.

"You know the deal," one of them said to him.

"Quiet," another whispered.

The ten-year-old boy was shaking so hard that he couldn't help but make some noise on the way up.

"All right, I'm here," he said, "I don't see anything."

One of the boys grabbed the opportunity to push his comrade through the doorway and then blocked the door. The poor ten-year-old screamed like he was being tortured in there. All the kids laughed and ran up to hear better.

"Let me out, please," he begged, "It's in here! It's here!"

"Hey!" Alex yelled at them.

Most jumped at his voice and ran away. One boy opened the door for his friend inside.

"Get out of here," Alex threatened and walked toward them. They knew better than to mess with a late teen, and ran, some of them still mocking their friend.

Alex walked through the doorway, hoping his brother wasn't inside. "You there, Hen?"

He heard a stifled breath, and a sniff like someone had been crying. "Yes," came a cracked voice from somewhere in the dark.

"I'm sorry," Alex said.

"For what?"

"I could've stopped those boys."

"It's fine. I'm used to it."

"I just came to say hi," Alex said, looking around, but then he realized Henry was only a few yards in front of him, just an outline in the shadows. "How's the Sun feeling?"

"Stings still."

"That why you haven't left?"

"You don't know I haven't left."

"Well just in case," Alex said, "I brought food," and handed him a chocolate bar.

Henry took the gift. "You didn't have to spend money on me."

"Well, I wasn't gonna steal it."

Henry chuckled.

"I got a scholarship that allows some extra food money."

"Wow, so you're all in now. Good job," he chewed the candy bar.

"I've looked into your condition at the University."

"Stop Alex, you were supposed to forget that."

"I won't forget. I talked to some professors. This guy, Dr. Leonard, was really interested."

"Who cares that he's interested?"

"Well, he thinks there's a possibility."

"No, Alex, I can't do this again."

"He said that in a lot of cases of discolored skin, the blood is what causes it."

"So?"

"So if we change your blood, we could get your skin better."

"I have no shadow! How can they fix that?"

"I don't know, but wouldn't it be better than nothing? Don't you want to try?"

"No."

"Henry."

"I've finally accepted that this is how I am. I can't hope for anything better, and that's okay."

"Come on, I know there's a way."

"Shut Up! I can't hope anymore. It's ruined me."

"Sorry, I'll drop it, but can you do me a quick favor?" He took out a syringe, "I just need some blood, then you can forget it forever."

"Fine," he said and held his arm out. Alex clumsily stuck the needle in.

"Sorry, I gotta go," Alex said after the blood was drawn, and he ran off, looking at the thin, black blood of his kin.

Dr. Leonard needed to work fast to test the blood Alex brought back to the laboratory. All he needed to know was Henry's blood type, so it didn't take very long.

"It's B," the professor said.

"Same as me," Alex said.

"Now we just need the volunteer."

"I can do it," Alex said.

"Don't take this the wrong way, Alex, but you seem a bit skinny for what we need. It'll take a lot of blood."

"You said yourself no one is going to want to do this. It's a new procedure, not proven and risky. I'm the only one who's going to volunteer."

The doctor laughed, "You'll be amazed at what people will do for a little cash these days."

"No," said Alex, "I'm not going to risk a stranger's life for this. He's my brother, it's my responsibility."

"You realize that this could even kill you. You only have ten pints of blood in you, and we'd need at least four," said Dr. Leonard. Alex nodded. "Ok, if you say so," he agreed, "This'll work out better anyway, I would be somewhat shunned by the medical community if this was done publicly. Not to mention blood transfusion is not completely legal yet."

Alex confirmed, and they shook hands.

"Great, then I'll see both of you back here next Wednesday at ten, and it'll all be ready for you. And good luck on that paper in Smith's. He can be quite harsh on grammar," he winked.

"Thanks," Alex took off to find Henry.

* * *

He went to Murphey's Mill again, but it was quiet and empty when he walked inside.

"It's me," he finally said, and a shadow shifted towards him.

"Hi," said Henry.

"I know you don't want to get your hopes up, but Professor Leonard said he would perform a special process that could cure you."

"That's impossible. You're fooling yourselves."

"No, it's true. People have already been cured of blood diseases."

"I don't want to try, Alex."

"Why? Because you think it won't work, or you don't want to be better."

"Of course I want to get better."

"Then shouldn't you at least try this? What do you have to lose?"

Henry thought about it. "Nothing I haven't already lost, I guess."

"Exactly. We need to be there next Wednesday."

"So what's the procedure? Why'd he need a needle of my blood?"

"To check your blood type. There are four different blood types that we all have. It's called a blood transfusion, and it's where we take someone else's blood and put it into you, but you have to have the same blood type for that to work."

"That doesn't sound too bad."

"No, but at the same time we'd have to drain your blood."

"How much of it?"

"About half for your body to start producing the new blood rather than the old."

"Who's going to give me the new blood?"

"I'm the obvious candidate."

"What? Are you joking?"

"It's fine, I'll just give you four pints, that's forty percent. I can handle it."

"No, you can't. How can you be wanting this?"

"How are you refusing? You can be cured! Wouldn't you give anything for that?"

"No, I wouldn't, not risking your life."

"It's worth it to me."

"How? How is it worth it? You would do this just so I could look normal?"

"Yes, I've seen my brother get spit on and hated for eighteen years, and I've had enough."

"Just let me be. So what, I hate myself, I'm basically a ghost. I've been living with it this entire time. I'm fine."

Alex just looked sad. "But you're not fine," he said, "I don't want to admit it, but you're less of yourself every time I see you."

"I'm not going to let you do this," Henry said.

"Well, I'm not letting you sit here anymore in your

self-pity until you kill yourself."

Henry was silent, and still. Tears welled up in his eyes, which was confirmation enough.

"I'm going to the clinic tomorrow," said Alex, "and I'm bringing you with me, conscious or unconscious. You want to stop me, do it now."

Henry accepted his brother's offer and swung at his face. The fist made contact, and Alex almost fell over, but recovered and kicked Henry in the gut. Henry grabbed him, and they grappled to the floor. Alex got up first and managed to push Henry out the door into the sunshine. Henry screamed in pain and lunged back and threw Alex down the steps to the ground. The wind was clear knocked out of Alex, but he stood, wobbly, and charged back in. Henry had never seen Alex this determined about anything before. They continued tussling in the shadows until Alex was bleeding from his lip and had a black eye. Henry was in much better condition than his brother, but Alex wouldn't give up. Something in his eyes had changed.

"All right," Henry said, raising his hands, "We'll go."

Alex laughed and lowered his arms. Henry could not deny the small hope that rekindled inside of him. The painful, nostalgic, yet pleasant feeling that he'd almost forgotten.

In the morning, they both got up early and walked to the train station which took them to the University. All of Henry's skin was covered with clothing, but he still looked down the whole time, avoiding the glares of all the people sitting by them. Alex whispered, "This is the last time you're going to have to endure this."

When they entered the university laboratory, a few assistants were getting everything ready. Henry felt intimidated in the spacious room. It didn't look like it was meant to treat patients.

Finally, Dr. Leonard arrived. "Excuse my tardiness, gentlemen. Hello, Alex. And you must be Henry." He offered his hand to Henry. Stunned, Henry looked behind him, then back at the hand and cautiously shook it. Dr. Leonard laughed shortly. Alex would have laughed too if he didn't know Henry. "Shall we proceed?" Leonard motioned for them to sit, "This process will take a few hours."

Henry and Alex sat on their tall, skinny rolling gurneys. The two nurses, who were clearly still students, checked both of their pulses and blood pressures, then had them lie down while they brought the needles and tubes over. The two brothers exchanged a look that meant more than any words could have.

The needle was larger than Henry would have expected, and it stung when she slid it into his skin. One needle hooked into Alex's right arm, feeding blood into Henry's left, and another siphoned the blood out of Henry's right arm into a bucket on the floor. The blood rushing into his arm gave a weird sensation.

Henry admitted he felt different an hour in. The doctor said he did notice some changes. Alex was convinced of it, but the thought of being cured was too good to be true for Henry. In another hour, though, he saw Alex's face turned ghostly pale, and he forgot about himself.

"Is this ok?" he asked the professor.

"Yes, it's to be expected," the doctor consoled.

"I'm really fine," Alex said. They gave him water and blankets.

They talked through most of it, but by the halfway point, it was harder for Alex to concentrate enough to hold a conversation. He was closing his eyes, wanting to fall asleep. Twenty minutes later he could barely speak. His arm started to twitch, and soon his whole body was quivering.

"That's enough," Henry said, "He's had enough!"

"No" croaked Alex, and their arms kept draining.

Dr. Leonard even looked concerned now. One of the medical students felt his pulse for a full minute, and looked at him, "his pulse is slowing, but still stable."

Alex gave a last look at Henry and then fell asleep. A few minutes later, he looked so close to death, Henry couldn't take it anymore. He grabbed the needles to rip them out of his flesh, but the assistants restrained him.

"You still need more!" Leonard said.

"No! You're killing him," Henry shouted.

The door burst open suddenly, interrupting the conflict and revealing the last person on earth Henry expected to see. Frederick rushed over to Alex's table, and commanded, "You let my son go."

"You must be Mr. Miller," the doctor said, "but I'm

sorry, Alexander signed an agreement to this, and if we stop now, the procedure will fail."

"You must not have heard me."

"All of this will be in vain if–"

"Then I'll do it. I'll finish it. Take mine."

Leonard almost laughed, "A different blood type would kill him."

"I'm O negative."

"How would you know that? Blood types are hardly public knowledge yet."

"I studied a book and had the test done when Alex brought it home. I thought I might be the one to cure Henry."

A lump formed in Henry's throat.

Dr. Leonard considered it with his hand to his chin.

"Hurry up, man, or I'll do it myself."

"All right, all right, stop the flow from Alex," he told his students.

They immediately took out Alex's needle and bandaged his wound. One nurse felt his wrist again and looked at the others anxiously, "He's alive, but it doesn't look like he'll last."

"Give me two needles," Frederick said.

"As you wish. Get another table."

"No time, I can stand."

"Sir–"

"Just take my damn blood already,"

Dr. Leonard motioned to both assistants, "Bring a table here. You, get Mr. Miller's needles set up."

Frederick stood in between his sons' beds while the

nurses sanitized the new needles.

He stared at Alex for a few more moments, and then as if for the first time, he looked into Henry's eyes. Henry had never seen his father's face look so broken before.

"You," he started to say, but words were difficult for him, "…I'm so sorry."

Henry didn't know how to respond.

Frederick went on, "You were always my son."

Then they reconnected the needles, one in each of the man's arms, the dark red liquid rushing eagerly to both of his sons.

A table was brought which Frederick sat down on. He sat closer to Henry than Alex and reached out to grab the hand of his eldest.

"You were always my son."

Henry started to cry, but he did not understand why. This time he was crying for a different reason than he ever had before, and it felt good.

The students stopped bustling around, with nothing more to be done. Dr. Leonard sat and wrote in his logbook, every now and then looking up at them.

Henry and his father silently looked at Alex for a while.

"Will he be all right?" Fred finally asked.

"I think he will," replied the doctor, "I am very glad you came when you did."

Then Alex took the first audible breath in an hour. Henry thought he would never feel any lighter than he did at that moment. He stretched his hand out to his brother, and for the first time saw the new skin on it. There was just a hint of color. It was blotchy and faint, but definitely real. He started to chuckle, and soon couldn't do anything else but laugh.

A week later, they sat in a diner. Over the past week, Henry's skin gained more and more color. It was a full pink right now, which any normal man would have been embarrassed by, but he loved it. Compared to before, he was glowing. Dr. Leonard was surprised by this result and was feeling very good with himself. However, he could not hope to explain the other effect: Henry had a shadow now. There was no logical explanation for this, but Henry did not need one. All he knew was that before, he didn't truly believe that anyone loved him, and now he had proof that at least two people in the world did.

"How is it?" asked Alex, staring at the shadow Henry's hand was making on the table.

Henry looked at his arm, then back at them and shrugged, "Eh."

They all laughed again.

Night happened to glide by an apartment window a year later and didn't recognize Henry at her first glance. When she did, she didn't even say hello, but hovered outside his window for a time, enjoying what would be her new favorite sight. Henry was sitting on his bed alone, yet he was smiling. She giggled and flew off.

B.S.

Indeed, copper is not copper

And silver isn't silver
Money weighs as worthless

But worth-full are the looks.
Suppose we all could fly today
Into the shiny blue
Not many would dare float up and
Go see blue is black.

This black will always be black
His black will never
Isn't this why we pretend
So we'll still have our other?

Life is never good enough
Indecent is this thought, yet
Frequently we wish to join
Every soul who's passed.

Since diamond is not diamond
Only plastic tells the truth.

Many people do not
Understand me and you
Cold and hot are our hearts
How can we be heartless?

B.S.

I ndeed, copper is not copper

A nd silver isn't silver
M oney weighs as worthless

B ut worth-full are the looks.
S uppose we all could fly today
I nto the shiny blue
N ot many would dare float up and
G o see blue is black.

T his black will always be black
H is black will never
I sn't this why we pretend
S o we'll still have our other?

L ife is never good enough
I ndecent is this thought, yet
F requently we wish to join
E very soul who's passed.

S ince diamond is not diamond
O nly plastic tells the truth.

M any people do not
U nderstand me and you
C old and hot are our hearts
H ow can we be heartless?

ONIVER

I am not writing this to make money off of it, or to become famous or anything like that, I simply want to relate a story.

This is an old story that has been passed down through a very particular group of people who do not like sharing their heritage with others, so this is probably the first time you've heard of it. I felt the need to commit a bit of a taboo and get it into writing so that everyone can benefit from it before it is lost forever. Even if that does happen, and the story is destroyed with my people, I am not worried. The core of the story is something a lot of us already know. So, here is the story of Oniver.

It happened when civilization was first developing on our world. Life was simpler then, we can be sure, but by no means less intelligent. There was a society of people tucked away into one of the valleys, surrounded by mountains. Just one village, one tribe, disconnected from the rest of the world—my ancestors.

Something about them was very unusual, but this would possibly not be apparent to a casual observer. They farmed, fished, hunted, played, and sang much like any other people. One would have to stay with them for a time to see the extent of the strangeness.

At first, one would note the obvious fact that they were small, proportioned maybe ten percent shorter than most humans in the current world, and all of them skinnier than current standards would deem healthy. This would only be noteworthy if one also saw the vast amount of food that they consumed. It seemed that no matter how much fish, game, fruits, vegetables, and bread they ate, they were never truly full, and to gain any weight was rare. If one spent some days there and was used to the routine, one would also start to notice something odd about the way the moved. They did things deliberately, even cautiously. No time was wasted, no hint of idleness among them. Even with their naps, there was a curious purposefulness. There was a tiredness that could not be overlooked. Everyone, down to the young, muscular men, would have to take breaks and lie down throughout the day. Exhaustion seemed to plague them constantly day and night, interrupting their schedules, seeping into their muscles, aching their bones. They did well despite it, making the best of whatever this dilemma was.

But all of this could be ignored or rationalized in the mind until one had stayed with them for a year or two. Then one would have to acknowledge that the strange, faint wisps of dark smoke that rose from all the people once every few weeks was not a hallucination. And one would have viewed the same person who looked middle-aged the last year suddenly become elderly in that short time. The body more shriveled, hair whitened, voice choked and gravelly. One would wonder at this, and then notice that all the inhabitants also aged similarly. If one stayed for ten years, one would see that they died much sooner than they ought to have. The aging of the entire village was accelerated past any normal human. What sort of curse or degenerative disease could cause this?

One would have to travel up the mountains to find the answer. There one would find that there are those who are less human than most. Near the top of one mountain, in caves that had been carved and decorated over many years with rugs, paints, and fabrics, there resided another people. They lived a life of complete opposite to their neighbors. They would appear to do almost no work at all, but instead lounged, loved, talked, laughed, and most of all, drank. They would maybe finish mending a new set of clothes in a week, but that was it. Contrary to the bottom village, they hardly ever cooked or ate food, and yet every morning when they woke up, one might note that they appeared fatter, more refreshed, and even younger than the night before. Younger not quite in age, but in luster, vigor. And then they would begin their revelry once again. While some would not sleep for days at a time, their youthful manner would continue as all the others.

Underneath their pleasant joviality was something sinister. One might wish to take part in their feasts and parties, but a warning of the senses would likely prohibit participation. It seemed wrong, unnatural, in a way similar to the lower village, but a strikingly different manifestation. If one stayed longer, the mystery would begin to reveal itself. Once every month, all the citizens of these caves would gather together and put their heads down, silently focusing on some unseen object. Then something that looked like mist or smoke, but blacker, would appear from all directions, coming in through the walls, up from the ground, travelling in thin trails until it reached the people. If you can imagine what a stream of smoke exiting a smoker's mouth would look like if time was reversed, and the smoke entered into the mouth again using the same trail it exited from, then you can imagine what took place here. The entire bodies of everyone in this ritual breathed in the smoke, and who knows what it did once it was in them, because it would never come out again.

They absorbed the mist, taking it in like it was medicine. The process would last for about ten minutes, and then they would continue in their various revelries. This would make all other deeds committed by them seem less pleasurable, and more juvenile, not as in innocence or naivety but in maliciousness. Mature in the knowledge of evil.

Jezikri, the hero, is one who observed both societies as objectively as I have described them to you, only in the opposite order. But you will have to wait to meet him, as now we will meet our main character, who, like most real characters, is not the hero. Not in a heroic sense anyway, but Oniver was a decent enough man.

Each person in the lower village, including Oniver, was inflicted by the same curse. Their lives were cut short by three-quarters. Oniver was hardly past thirteen years old, one hundred and fifty-seven months by their count. A boy in our culture, but in theirs, he was married, and two-thirds of his life had already gone past. He had the body of a forty-year-old man. But his life would not have been so miserable if he had not known any better.

Sadly, Oniver knew all too well what his people had become, and what they used to be. He knew the stories of ten generations ago when everyone lived for so long that they counted in years— twelve-month intervals. It was not uncommon for someone's age to reach over one thousand months. These ancestors could work in the heat of the day and need no rest, and still have more energy for dancing at night. They could scale mountains, swim across lakes, and lift a whole buck over their shoulders alone. He knew what the Malums from the mountains took from them, and that he could never fight against them. Not one of the Malums had ever been known to die. Oniver knew that he was trapped here for the rest of his stunted life. He did not mind the idea of death so much, but had just been married the year before, and his beautiful wife had become pregnant. Then the tragedy of this life struck him, as it had struck his parents when he was born.

Under the warm, blue autumn sky, Oniver dwelt on these facts while he hoed the ground. They were all but forbidden from even thinking about their condition since it could take away from the energy of their work. But he could not stop. Why were he and his future children punished for his ancestor's folly? What had they done to deserve this? How could this curse be placed on them, what kind of magic were the Malums using? Why were his people powerless to defend themselves? These questions raged in his mind as he struck the earth with his fellow farmers. When the hour of rest came, at noon, exhausted and knowing that it was a foolish thing to do, he marched toward the House of Elders.

Someday, if Oniver was lucky enough to live past two hundred and forty months, he would have the honor of living in that house, and he too would counsel the tribe with the title Elder. He considered waiting until that age to attempt what he was about to, but by that time his child would be already forty months old, and how many of them would also die before then? No, he could not wait any longer.

The large, round, stone hut came into view. It was the only building in the village that was not made from wood, clay, and straw. He pushed open the intricately engraved oak door and walked into the dark room, waiting for his eyes to adjust.

"What are you doing here, Oniver?" came a stern voice that was recognized as Visair Elder.

"Honored elder, you know it is me, even though your eyes are bad."

"Who else could it be who comes in here during rest?"

"Visair, you woke me," came the feminine voice of Ella Elder.

"I am so sorry to intrude now," Oniver spoke, "But I require counsel."

Visair Elder laughed mockingly, "Or do you wish to counsel us again?"

"No, I only have questions to ask."

"All right, you may ask. I am sure Alabar Elder will wake and counsel you too if it is interesting enough to him."

Instead of asking any of the clever, well thought out questions he had been constructing over the last few days, Oniver simply blurted, "Why do you not care that we are dying? Is there really no way that we can be free?"

"Oniver, why do you harm yourself by asking such

questions?"

"Because I want to see my child grow to be happy and healthy and not die long before her rightful time."

"I see no reason that she should be unhappy, unless you instill in her the same ungratefulness that is in you. She will live like all of us, and sleep and eat and laugh and dance and sing and play, and then work, so many blessings."

"But all of those things are almost gone, compared to what they were many months ago. They have been stolen from us, and we are doing nothing to get them back."

"No, we cannot get our previous way of life back, we have learned that lesson. You know the history of when our ancestors fought one thousand months ago, and we paid dearly for it. Only a few were kept alive to be drained and to reproduce. And six hundred months ago, they attempted to escape the mountains, but this also failed. The Malums found out and again slaughtered many. And I know you do not remember, but the generation of my parents attempted a new strategy. Half of us marched up the mountain to fight, and half of us ran, to ensure that some would escape their power. But even this failed. All who chose to fight died and those who ran were crippled and maimed and put back here, our home. We are still recovering a suitable population from this, and we cannot risk endangering ourselves once more. I hope escape from this valley is never attempted again. We cannot be free. Giving a length of our lives to them is our price for being alive. Be grateful that you are alive."

"I am grateful, but not content. I am still curious how, and respect you for how you manage it."

"Simply accept your lot in life."

Ella Elder spoke, "Oniver, there are some things that we can change and some that we cannot. If this curse was not on you, you would still eventually die. Focus on changing what you can change to make the best life for the future."

"Yes, I will do that. Another question, is it impossible for us to use the same magic as the Malums are using?"

"You know the history, that their power comes from the great dragon, so it will not work for us who do not come from him."

"Could we not barter with this dragon, or the Malums, though we are enemies?"

"And trade something more valuable than your life mist, which they already possess? What else could you give them?"

"My body. My death."

The elder laughed, "They will take that, too."

"Oniver," said Ella Elder, "If you truly wish to go up the mountain and see for yourself, you have our blessing."

"No, you do not!" Visair said.

"Yes he does," Ella responded.

"Very well, but I forbid you to take anyone with you. Go, since your life is worth so little to you."

Oniver bowed, "I will go, but because my child's life

is worth more than my own."

"Do not die," Ella Elder said as he went out.

He felt confident and terrified while walking to his house, his father's house, and his father's father's house. Tara was not going to let him leave, he knew, but he still had to tell her. He opened the straw door as quietly as he could manage, hoping she was asleep.

"Where were you? You leave me to rest alone," Tara accused from their bed mat.

"I am sorry," he laid down next to her. "I was speaking to the Elders."

"It is the fifth time you skipped rest."

"Please try to sleep, for the baby. I am sorry."

"What did you ask them?"

"I will tell you everything later."

Oniver knew he needed to sleep more than she did before the journey, but even with his exhaustion, calming down was difficult. He turned his head to his wife and heard her breathing becoming regular, her belly moving up and down, a little larger than it was just a week ago. He knew it was ironic (if they had such a word back then) that the very thing that made him want to stay was the same thing that had forced him to go.

This cannot go on. Something must be done.

The bell signifying the evening rest startled him awake. He had slept through the whole afternoon. Tara was asleep beside him, but he noticed she had made soup while he was out. He stealthily put carrots, bread, and dried fish into a sack, and filled a pouch with water, then debated on whether or not to take the extra cloak. The mountains would be cold, but the extra weight would make it more straining. He decided to leave it.

Tara stirred, yawned, and mentioned, "Did I sleep past the bell?" but then she saw what he was doing and sprung up to her feet. "No, Oniver, no. You are not serious."

Oniver looked disappointed in himself, but said, "I am. The Elders gave me their blessing. I will go make a way for us."

"No, you cannot go," She shouted and snatched his bag from him and started to remove the items he collected.

"I know you want to be free as badly as I do."

"It is not worth your life, please think of our child."

"It was the thinking of our child that brought me to this decision."

"Do not throw away your life for this! If not for yourself, or your baby, then for me."

"My love," he said and hugged her tightly. "Every decision I have made for this last year was for you and our child. I must go, with or without your blessing."

She cried in his arms, and then sat down and refused to look at him.

"Tara," he said, but she kept her head turned.

She continued her silence toward him while he finished packing that night, and in the early morning when he kissed her cheek and said farewell.

He walked outside, struck down, but not destroyed, perplexed, but not despairing. He was glad he did not run into any other people on the way out, not wanting to explain himself to them also. Soon he was entering the forest. He knew that he had better pray to the Creator, though he had not prayed much in his lifetime. All he could think to say was, "Please do not let me die. I want to see my child's face."

There was no path to follow up the mountain, but he knew he would reach the peak if he went straight up the side, through this forest. That is the way they came down at least. The Malums were bigger, younger, and more aggressive than any of his tribe, no one could stop them from doing what they wanted.

The beasts rarely killed any of them on purpose, being the source of their food and life, but they liked to stand near the camp and joke about how his people were like cattle. Occasionally one would take a young, screaming girl or boy from the village, who would never be seen again, but this was rare. The general opinion those monsters expressed toward the lower village was disgust, a mutual feeling.

Oniver's hatred of them fueled his march for the first few miles, but by then he was exhausted. He rested and ate there under a tree, and almost fell asleep, but stopped himself, wanting to reach the lair before nightfall. After he felt rejuvenated enough, with half the water ashamedly depleted, he pressed on.

It was during the next mile that the doubts came. He was making a grave mistake. The Malums would kill him, no question. He pushed the thoughts out of his mind and kept going. Legs burned more with each step, and soon it seemed impossible for him to catch his breath. Even in the cold air, he was sweating. Soon the tired man stopped and looked around and noticed that the landscape looked no different than it did at the bottom. He was getting nowhere. What had caused him to make such a foolish decision? What change could he possibly bring to his people? He was throwing away his life for no reason, just like they had said.

He turned around and started walking back down, destroyed and despairing. After about a mile, he dropped down to give his lungs a rest, and then cried. He wept like the little ones do, not the gentle crying of Tara. He had been a fool. Then he gulped the rest of his water and fell asleep.

When he came to his senses, he stood up but did not start walking immediately. He deliberated more, then understood that he had to turn around again and go back up the mountain. He had already made up his mind to do so before he left. The only options were to keep moving forward or to give up and assign the same fate to his child.

Grabbing a firm stick for support, he pressed up the mountain once more, muscles burning with every step. He thought about stopping for the night, but he knew the chances of a Malum finding him would only increase the longer he was there. When the sun's light was dimming at evening, the trees began to grow scarcer, and the air was colder and thinner than in the lower elevation. He was getting closer. Hope filled his heart, but his lungs hurt with each gasp, and his heart was beating faster than it ever had before. The farther he pushed, the closer he felt to death. Every cell of his body was in rebellion against his will, but still, he went forward until he could not move anymore.

Once again, he sank to his hands and knees and wept, this time to the Creator.

"Please," he screamed in between breaths, "Please give me the strength to move forward. They have taken everything from us! So much is gone. Please return the life they stole. It is our birthright, to be free. Give it back to us!"

More energy surged inside of him, and he pushed himself up again, determined to not waste any. He did not try to wonder whether this was Creator answering his prayer or not. The only thing occupying his mind was putting one leg forward, and then the other one. And then he was in a clearing of trees, and face to face with a cliff. A hole, arch-shaped and neatly carved, could be seen clearly in the moonlight. He was too weak and cold to consider caution as he hobbled inside the dark. The relief from the wind was immediate, and he sat down and fell asleep.

A jolt of fear woke him as if he realized in his sleep what a foolish decision it was to nap there. Gathering the wits that had abandoned him during the strenuous journey, he considered his plan. He thought he would sneak past as many of the Malums as he could, and try to determine the source of their power, perhaps this dragon if it existed, or get one of the Malums alone, so he could either bargain and plead for their lives, or kill it. He knew he would very likely die, no matter what he chose to do next, so the thought of killing one gave him an immense amount of satisfaction. There was a sharpened knife in his belt just for this purpose.

As the acknowledgment of his fate settled in his mind, a last pleading prayer for courage and favor was whispered, and a last lingering look at the blue trees and rocks outside the cave mouth was had. And then he stood up and turned toward the utter blackness of the cave. Walking slow enough for him to just barely hear his footsteps, he continued until he saw a sliver of light, and heard echoes of various noises. Then he continued slower and came to a dark curtain that allowed light to slip past its edges. An odd choice of doors, he thought, but then the Malums did not have much to fear from intruders. The noises then could be distinguished clearly as voices talking and metal dropping and glasses clinking. Should he go back and find another way in? He decided to at least see what was on the other side of this curtain. Trying to slow his breathing as much as possible, he grasped the fabric with a shaky hand and peeled open a crack to peek through.

It was a very large room, much different from the previous cave. Malums were everywhere, swarming the place. He heard much laughter—a kind that made him sick—jesting, yelling, and drinking, all echoing throughout the large cavern. And the smells almost made him vomit right there, the musty, wet smell of the cave mixed with food that had gone bad and a hint of human excrement. All their clothes and furniture and all around the walls were filled with vibrant colors, one of which he had never seen before, a deep sort of blue, or maybe more red. The light from torches was dim, probably enough for him to sneak along the back edge of the wall without being noticed. All of the Malums seemed consumed with whatever they were doing. Some looked like they were very close to making love right there in the open.

Looking farther to his left, he saw another curtain leading presumably to another hall. He knew that past this curtain, there would be no turning back, but he also knew there would likely not be a better chance than this. Girding himself up, he slid through into the warm room.

He was still at first, and only crept along the wall when he was certain not one had spotted him.

The Malums continued all their activities, and he continued crouching toward the curtain. It was only three yards away when he heard a shout.

"Hey, it's a Quart! over there."

Some of them did not even look up from what they were engaged with, but most turned to Oniver, either in surprise or with a weird smile. He raced to the curtain to escape, but a body moved in front of him. They were fast. Soon a crowd of Malums was gathered around him, blocking any hope of escape.

"What is it doing here?" one snarled with yellowed teeth.

"I come in peace," Oniver said in a surprisingly

stable voice.

"Shut up!" one of them yelled and slapped him so hard that he tumbled over. "Who told you to speak?"

Oniver regained as much dignity as he could while on the ground, "I wish to speak with whoever is willing."

"Did you not just hear me?" the Malum said and stomped on his hand.

Oniver reacted faster than any of them expected. He pulled out his knife and sliced the Malum's leg. It squealed like a pig. Oniver had only a moment to smile before the knife was pried out of his hand and he was grabbed and flung through the air. He was an entire ten feet above the ground before being slammed onto the hard floor again. These beings were even stronger than he had anticipated. He was unable to move.

The one whom he had injured squatted down next to him, and instead of using the knife, the Malum dug into his skin with its fingernails. They laughed as he showed more pain.

"I want to drain him, I want to drain him," a smaller female pleaded.

"He's almost gone anyways, not worth the effort," the yellow-toothed one said, and kicked Oniver's ribs until they cracked.

More of them laughed and joined in, kicking, stomping, and scraping his flesh. Each attack felt more violent than the last. A blank space started closing in around his vision, and he was sure he would die soon.

"Stop!" A voice commanded from the back of the

room.

The Malums stopped beating him, but he was too far gone to appreciate the change.

The voice continued, "I am taking this man with me."

"Why would we listen to you?" A measly voice countered.

"Don't listen to the traveler," Yellow Teeth said, "he's next."

"No," the traveler's voice said, "Kill me first."

A series of oohs and giggles wound through the crowd.

"All right, if you wish to die so much."

"Aw, but we were going to take our time with it later," the measly one complained.

"We can all drain a little," Yellow Teeth said, "I'll go first."

"Fine, then I am second!"

Oniver turned his head enough to see the commotion. All of them waited in anticipation as the Malum prepared itself to perform the draining. The man stood unworried as if he knew exactly what was happening. Soon the first embers of his life started to lift from him, but this also did not change his stance. When there was more of the mist about them, Oniver could see the clear green color in it, very unlike the dark grey or black from the villagers.

The Malums noticed too and were licking their greedy lips at its beauty. When it finally entered the yellow-toothed Malum, something happened that none of them, except possibly the traveler, had expected. It started gagging and shaking. Clearly in pain, it ceased the flow of mist from the man. The pain appeared to only increase, and the Malum flopped onto the ground, clutching its gut and convulsing. A piercing scream finally came out of its mouth that hurt Oniver's ears until it stopped moving, and then everything was still for some moments.

"Poison!" one screamed, "It's poisoned."

They all scattered away from the man, who then resumed his walk toward Oniver.

"Are you awake?" the man asked when he reached him.

Oniver nodded his head.

"Then let us get you out of here," the man put his arm underneath his shoulder and pulled him to his feet.

Oniver was barely able to put any pressure on his legs, but he managed to limp with the man's help toward to the curtain.

"You will pay for this," they heard a shout behind them, "you will all pay."

"Do not worry about them," the man said as they exited the cave.

The Malums did not follow them like Oniver expected them to. Not even one came to get revenge that whole night. They were walking down for a while before Oniver broke the silence with something other than his coarse breathing and winces. "Who are you?"

"Oh, you can talk," the stranger laughed. "You are better off than I thought. Still, you should rest and sleep soon."

"No," he said in between breaths, "if I do not return tonight, my wife will think I am dead."

"All right, we can continue. To answer your question, I am Jezikri. Probably an odd-sounding name to your language."

The man's way of speaking was odder than his name, but Oniver could understand him well enough. "What—what are you?"

He laughed, "I am a man, like you, but I am not from this country."

"What did you do to that Malum back there?"

"Oh, is that what you call them? Malum, I like that, an apt sounding name for the brutes. That Malum killed himself. What you saw him take from me is called Dobro. It is what I am made from. And he clearly did not have the stomach for it."

Oniver's eyes widened in wonder. "What were you doing there?"

"I might ask you the same question," Jezikri said. "I was traveling, hence their name for me, and they invited me in for a meal. I was hungry, so I obliged. They really do have some gross practices, but I was not about to judge their characters on their culture alone. When I saw them mistreating you, I knew they were corrupt. They were likely intending on killing me all along. So why were you there?"

Oniver realized he was strangely feeling well enough to talk fully. "I was there because my people are trapped, slaves to the Malums. The ritual they tried to perform on you, they do to us every month and it takes away our life. Most of our energy, our time, everything is drained from us. I was going there to try and learn how they do it, and try to trade with them, or stop them, or at least kill one."

Jezikri laughed again, "What a foolish thing to do. But a brave thing. I admire that."

"And I found you! You are our answer. Can you teach us how to have this 'Dobro' so we can defend ourselves against it?"

"I am sorry, but that is impossible." He stopped and thought. "At least, no it is not so simple."

"But there must be something you can do to help us. This was the reason I found you."

"You cannot learn Dobro as you learn a skill. It must be part of you. I will do what I can to help."

They talked about much more on their trip down to the village, which felt so different and much shorter to Oniver than his journey up. Jezikri asked him about his family, his tribe, his favorite food, and even got him to laugh at times. Oniver could not remember the last time he had laughed—really laughed—because to laugh for real is to be happy. More than that, every minute they spent together made Oniver feel more energized and soothed his wounds. He felt as if he were seventy months old again, a young man.

When they arrived at the village, it must have been very late because only the watchman, Kan, was awake.

"Oniver," the guard said, "Tara told me to watch for you, but I didn't think… how are you alive?"

"Hello, Kan," was all Oniver replied with, enjoying the look of bewilderment on the man's face.

Jezikri accepted Oniver's invitation of hospitality and was led to his house. Tara was awake when they walked in, sitting in her chair facing the door. To use words like ecstatic, overjoyed, relieved, elated, or even frenzied, would not describe her emotions from seeing her husband walk through her door again, but since there are not many other options in the English language, we will have to stick to those. She hugged and kissed him, ignoring whatever guest he had or hadn't brought with him until she had had enough, and then remembered how angry she should have been with him.

She made him tell her everything that happened before even acknowledging Jezikri, and then they settled down and she blessed Jezikri for his help and made them some tea. By the time the tea was done, they all realized how very tired they all were, so they laid out an extra mat for Jezikri and went to sleep.

When Oniver awoke, Tara was still asleep, but Jezikri was not in the house. He sprang up, hoping his mysterious savior had not left in the night.

He found Jezikri talking to Matta and Balti, who had been fishing. They were all laughing when Oniver came near.

"Oniver, you already know Matta and Balti, don't you?" Jezikri asked him.

"Of course," he said, taken aback.

Matta was still laughing, and asked, "Oniver, where

did you find this man?"

"With the Malums," he said, which shut her up quick. He turned to Jezikri, "I need to take you to our Elders."

"Very well. You mean right now?"

"No, they are asleep now, but I must ask you to not leave until then."

"Fear not, how could I leave when I have just arrived. The air is so pleasant here, and all the leaves green, and you have so graciously accepted me into your home, and I have already met two of your brothers and sisters. I would love to meet the rest, and I will perhaps depart after that."

"I must work, but I will find you when it is time for us to speak to the Elders."

"I will work with you," Jezikri beamed.

"No, please, you have done so much for me already. Enjoy yourself, you are our guest."

"All right," he said and sat down next to Balti.

Oniver went to work in his field, confident that Jezikri would not be able to meet the entire tribe and leave before the fourth hour. But by the third hour, Jezikri had already introduced himself to most of the village. He knew there would be no way to control this man. He was happy about how well the villagers took to him, though. It did not seem possible for anyone to dislike the stranger. There was a certain way in which he interacted with everyone that seemed equally concerned with each individual, yet unique to them all. It was like he knew their minds from just the first few words they would say.

Oniver could not deny the effects walking with Jezikri had on him, either.

"Eh, Oniver," Tampi, called to him while they worked, "I've had to take more breaks then you today. What has your wife been feeding you?"

"I suppose you're just getting older, Tampi."

When the bell rang, Oniver rushed to the new celebrity and brought him to the center of the village.

"Don't you want some food? You must be hungry," Jezikri said.

"That can wait," Oniver said when they were in front of the Elder house. He waited to catch his breath, and the pushed open the smooth door.

Hanra was there, feeding them breakfast.

"Oniver," Ella Elder said, "Is that you, are you alive?"

"Of course it is not Oniver," said Visair Elder.

"It is me," he said.

"What?" said Visair, "You are alive? Oh, you did not even reach the mountain. You turned back. Tell me this is what happened."

"No, I did go up the mountain, into the caves of the Malums."

"Then tell us how it is you are alive."

"I was saved. I found the cave and the Malums and attempted to reason with them, but they only wanted to inflict pain on me. I was sure that I would die, but then this man saved me," he gestured to his guest.

"My name is Jezikri, hello," and then he bent his

torso over forwards, but kept his legs straight.

They did not react well to this, but you try to imagine seeing someone bow to you for the first time and not laugh.

"How did this man save you?" asked Visair.

"He is a stranger who was traveling across the mountain, and Malums invited him in, in order to drain him. When he told them to stop hurting me, they started the draining. What came out of Jezikri into the Malum killed it and scared all the others away."

"This man came from the Malums' caves and you bring him here? How dare you."

"Hush Visair, listen to yourself," Ella Elder said, "Thank you, stranger. We are in your debt for saving Oniver."

"There is no debt," he replied.

Visair shouted, "He is a spy sent to harm us even more."

"Even more," Ella almost laughed, "How could that even be possible. What more could be done to us?"

"Don't you realize what this means?" Oniver could not contain himself, "The Malums can die! I've seen it with my own eyes."

"Wait," Jezikri said, "I never killed anyone, that Malum, as you call them, killed himself. I am not about to wipe out an entire population for you."

"I knew it," Visair said, "The only one who wouldn't want the Malums dead would be one of them."

"I am not one of them!"

Visair looked smug, "So whose side are you on then? Ours or theirs?"

"I am on neither, of course," Jezikri stated. But he looked at Oniver's hopeless face, and said, "I may be able to help you still."

"How?" Oniver asked.

"I believe I am able to reverse the effects of the draining. I can make you like I am."

"But on the mountain, you said that could not happen."

"I said it was not simple."

"And how are you so confident?" Visair asked.

"Because I already tried it on Oniver."

"What?" Visair said.

"On the way down the mountain, I gave some of my Dobro to him to heal his wounds. Though I fear this is only temporary a temporary solution. Can you deny that he already looks more rejuvenated than when he left?"

"It is true," Oniver said, "I feel much better. Younger, and all my wounds were healed. I could not understand why at the time."

"I do not accept it," Visair Elder said, "Nor can I trust that you will not in some way harm us."

"I am evidence," said Oniver, "trust me."

"They only want to give us more so they can drain it again."

"Even if that were true," Jezikri addressed Visair Elder, "And the only purpose of me being here was to trick you into giving more to them, would it not still be worth it, to see how life was meant to be? Do you not desire at least one day of this?"

"No, I would rather not know what I am missing."

"I would like to know," said Ella Elder. "I would like to experience a different life for a moment, but I am sorry that I agree with Visair. This offer is very tempting, but Visair's caution may be our protection against things we cannot see, as it has been in the past."

"This is our only chance!" Oniver said.

"No, we will not tolerate more disruptions in our life cycle," said Visair.

While they were arguing, no one noticed a green mist coming out from Jezikri, heading toward Alabar Elder. Of the three current members of the house of Elders, Alabar Elder was the oldest, at three hundred and three months. Ten months ago, he lost the function of his ears and eyes, and his voice was nearly inaudible. The only sign that he was alive was the faint wheezing noises he made, and the fact that he still ate food. Since the previous month, he had not spoken a single word, and the wheezing had grown worse.

The mist was trailing around the room, winding its way toward Alabar Elder's seat, and no one saw it enter into his body. He did not move or make a sound at first, but then he stirred and coughed.

This was enough to stop the argument and turn every head to the dying old man. He coughed again and again, getting louder. Hanra, who had been feeding him, tried to soothe him any way she could. Then they all saw the green smoke snaking from Jezikri into the elder.

"Stop," Visair yelled at him, "Stop this immediately!"

Jezikri had his eyes closed and did not obey.

Ella looked stunned. Even Oniver was concerned. Alabar Elder did not stop shaking.

"Someone! Help," Visair shouted.

Oniver heard footsteps running toward the door, and soon a few men burst through. At that moment, Alabar opened his eyes and stopped coughing, and then the flow of green ended. The cough from the Elder was replaced by smooth, deep breaths. He sat up straight and looked at them all one-by-one. There was an intelligence to his eyes that had not been there for a long time.

Tampi started to say, "What's the matter," but he stopped when something even more remarkable happened. A gentle, deliberate voice sounded that they all recognized.

"Would anyone happen to have a cup of water on hand?" Alabar Elder said.

Hanra quickly obliged the request.

"Oh, thank you Hanra."

"What happened?" Tampi said.

"Jezikri," answered Oniver. He noticed Jezikri was trying to hide his hard breathing, and a sweat bead dripped down his face.

The next day Alabar looked as young as the other Elders, and the day after that he looked younger.

Everyone wanted to know how Jezikri did this and wanted a piece of it for themselves. Even Visair was almost convinced. But Jezikri denied them, saying, "After I give the Dobro to you, I must leave. I want to enjoy life with all of you here first."

And he did just that. Life went on for the next few weeks just as it had been, only they were all excited for the coming days, not dreading them as usual. People worked and sang, children played, and Jezikri worked and sang and played with them. When speaking with adults, he would demonstrate as much knowledge as any of them, but when playing with the kids, he would act like he was no older than they. He would spend at least an entire day with just one family, and then move on to the next.

Even the Elders respected him and enjoyed discussing almost any topic together since he was even older and more experienced than they were. Alabar Elder had a special bond with him, and they talked like old friends.

After a few weeks had passed, Jezikri was sitting with Oniver, overlooking the village. The climb up the hill was difficult for Oniver. Just like Jezikri had predicted, he had lost the youthfulness that he had recently gained from him. He noticed the hero's face looked sad, and his voice did not try to hide it.

"I have known everyone, all of your family for long enough now. It is time for me to go."

"But everyone loves you here. Why would you leave? Why not stay and live with us, and you could keep healing us, too."

"That is the reason I am going. I have decided to heal all of you fully so that the Malums cannot harm you or your future generations. You will all be safe."

"Really," Oniver's face lightened again at the prospect, "but you said that you could not make it permanent, and my energy has faded as before like you predicted."

"Yes, it is as I feared. Putting some Dobro in you did not change what you are. I must give to you completely, empty myself."

Oniver spent a bit of time trying to figure out what he meant, then gave up.

Jezikri continued, "I will give away all of my Dobro to you so that there is none left for me. That is the only way to change you so that they cannot touch you."

"And you could do this all along?"

"I will die."

All Oniver could respond with was, "No."

"I will die, but you will be free."

"No, you cannot. You cannot!"

"It is my choice to make. I love you, your whole tribe."

"But, is this really the only way? Then don't give me your Dobro. I can die soon, I have accepted that. Give it to Tara, not me."

"Oniver, your whole life you have had a passion to be free, accept it now. If I was to give my whole life for one person, it would kill me just the same as for the whole tribe."

"I want freedom at the cost of the Malums' lives, not an innocent life!"

"No, you desire either freedom or revenge. You cannot desire both."

"Freedom, then."

Jezikri laughed, "I am happy about this. After my body is gone, I will still be alive, and you will see me again."

Oniver did not understand these things, but he saw that Jezikri still did not look happy. They both cried as they walked down to the village.

Jezikri went to the center of the village, the House of Elders, and told Oniver to bring the entire tribe there. Then he went inside and even convinced the Elders to come out and listen to him, too.

People asked Oniver why, but he could not bring himself to tell them. He only said, "Jezikri wants to see you."

Jezikri was kneeling with his eyes closed as they gathered. Old and young faces were there, and soon the entire village was packed tightly around him, anticipating what he was going to tell them. When he stayed quiet and unmoving, Visair Elder spoke.

"Let me tell you all our history again. We were once a great people. Joyful and prosperous, and living with our Creator, but we did not like the land he had chosen for us, so we left. Our ancestors traveled long until they found this valley. Lush and green and plentiful, we found it to be the perfect place to establish our new home. But we did not know of the monsters that lived in the mountains, and as soon as we finished building our homes, we felt their effect. At first, we thought it was a disease, but then we explored and discovered the Malums and their magic, and by then it was too late. We were slaves to their curse. We attempted to flee and to fight for our justice, but we did not succeed. We prayed to Creator, but he did not answer because we had left him. For two thousand months, we have been forced to give three-fourths of our lives to the Malums. And now, finally, a man has been sent to us and has shown us a glimpse of the life we had lost. Please, listen with me to Jezikri, who has power over the curse."

Everyone was silent and waited again for Jezikri.

He opened his eyes and finally spoke. "I came from the very Creator that you speak of, and I am going back. I love you and am glad to have known each one of you. This is why I am deciding to give you a gift before I leave. The curse on you can be broken, your hopes are true. It is how you will choose to live after this that I am curious about."

"You cannot stay here with us?" Tara asked.

"No," tears started coming from his eyes again, "What I am going to give you will—will cost me my life."

"What?" some people stammered and started making objections.

"I have made up my mind, and I did not come to this decision lightly. My death in exchange for your freedom. It is a fair trade, and now that I know you all, I would be a horrible friend if I did nothing to help you."

"Jezikri don't go!" a child said.

"Come closer," he said, "all of you." They all took steps closer, encircling him. The child sat on his lap. "Please," he continued, "please let me heal you. Nothing would make me happier."

Alabar Elder, who could not walk easily, came over and put a hand on his shoulder, tears coming from his eyes, too. "My friend, I cannot thank you enough. I will accept your gift, only because I know you would have sacrificed yourself whether we agreed to it or not."

No one else objected.

"And I will live again," Jezikri said, "I am going to my home through death, but you can come there through life. You will all be able to find me. Now, just rest. You do not need to do anything, only do not run."

He took in a deep breath. All they could hear were each other crying and waiting. Then all at once, hundreds of streams of the green mist shot out from him. The streams twisted and turned and found their way to each person. It was an undeniably beautiful sight while it lasted, but no one was able to enjoy it. Jezikri was in obvious pain.

Everyone felt the effects of the Dobro immediately. Most of them dropped to the ground, overwhelmed by the change. It did not feel bad at all, but there are some things that are so good as to be shocking, even terrifying. The instant relief of any tiredness, ached bones, sore muscles, cuts, and bruises was too much to comprehend.

Jezikri collapsed on the ground, soundless, but the green streams did not stop. About a minute later, the last wisps of smoke lifted from him and dissolved into the people. He never took another breath. When people got their wits about them, they did not celebrate their newfound life, but stared at his lifeless body.

He was buried in their most honored grave, reserved for elders. For years there was always at least one person standing there, remembering Jezikri.

Just a few days after his sacrifice, everyone noticed trails of smoke coming up from them once again, heading toward the mountain. It was now green, not black. They all smiled at each other, knowing what this meant. The next day, Oniver decided to lead an expedition up the mountain once more. There was no real reason, now that they were unaffected by the curse, but many people still desired to go with him.

They brought their bows and arrows along, just in case, a party of about twenty. Oniver found that the hike up the mountain was not difficult at all, and it took them just three hours instead of a whole day and night to reach the top. Oniver found the same cave he was in before, and they followed him boldly, unafraid at whatever would meet them on the inside.

Dead bodies of Malums were strewn throughout all the caves they explored. It was a disgusting sight, but the group could not help but laugh about it with each other. Tampi stumbled upon three Malums that were still alive, huddled together in a room.

He wanted to kill them, but Oniver remembered

what Jezikri told him about freedom and revenge, so he decided to bind them and take them back to the village.

"I hate you! You will pay for this! I can't wait to kill you!" the Malums kept saying.

They did their best to ignore them.

At the bottom, they put them into cages to keep them from leaving and hurting other people. They even gave them food and water. The Malums greedily consumed whatever they were given, but their bodies had adapted to needing life mist more than physical food, and they all died within a few days.

After that, anything pleasant, joyful, celebratory, or worthy of praise, they called 'dobro.' And anything wrong, negative, or painful, they called 'malum.' These words are translated into English as 'good' and 'evil.' This is where those opposites came from, according to my ancestors.

§

The reason why humans love symmetry so much is because nature loves symmetry. The reason why nature loves symmetry is because it was created to.

§

Stories all have symmetries
To me they do, anyway
On every script, novel, or poem
Ranging from every form
In every varying culture
Eternal patterns exist
Soaking into the air
Active even in graffiti
No storyteller can escape
Directions of human lives

S	tories all have symmetrie	S
T	o me they do anywa	Y
O	n every script, novel, or poe	M
R	anging from every for	M
I	n every varying cultur	E
E	ternal patterns exis	T
S	oaking into the ai	R
A	ctive even in graffit	I
N	o storyteller can escap	E
D	irections of human live	S

THE END

A Request to the Reader

Thank you for buying this book! These days, it is extremely difficult to sell many books as a self-published author, and it is impossible without support from readers. Now that you've finished reading, please consider helping me out by leaving a review online about this book, and by joining my Facebook page, Josh's Bookshelf.

www.ingramcontent.com/pod-product-compliance
Lightning Source LLC
Chambersburg PA
CBHW021054130626
46552CB00005B/2089